MISADVENTURES

WITH A

TWIN

MISADVENTURES

WITH A

TWIN

BY
ELIZABETH HAYLEY

WATERHOUSE PRESS

ISBN: 978-1-64263-160-9

To Meredith, for always being in our corner

CHAPTER ONE

COLTON

"I can't believe we're actually going to this thing," Corey said as he zipped up his jacket and exited my truck. "Why's it so cold this weekend?"

"Um...because it's Boston in November," I said. I closed my door and ran to catch up with him on the sidewalk. "We've lived here all our lives. You should be used to this."

"I'm used to being at home. Let's go there instead," he said, turning toward me.

Except for his pathetic expression that was silently pleading with me to let him off the hook, it was like looking in a mirror. Dark hair with cropped sides—long enough to style on top but short enough that we didn't have to—and dimples that were noticeable even when we weren't smiling, causing elderly women to call us cute like they would a baby in a grocery store line. Even after almost thirty years, it was tough for most people to tell us apart.

"I can't understand why you haven't had a date in a couple of months. You're a blast," I said dryly. "Aren't you supposed to be the friendlier one?"

"It's just that we haven't talked to most of these people in years. It's weird."

I rubbed my hands together to get them warm. Corey was

right. It was freezing tonight. "That's why we're here. We can talk about all the crazy shit we used to do."

He raised an eyebrow at me. "You *still* do crazy shit."

"Okay, so we'll tell everyone about all the new crazy shit." Corey rolled his eyes and laughed.

"Come on, you know it'll be fun." I wrapped an arm around his neck and pulled him toward me to mess up his hair so I would look better than him.

Corey laughed as he broke free of my hold and put an arm out in front of my chest to stop me. He raised his eyebrows at me, and then somehow—like we used to when we were kids—we telepathically counted to three and then took off at full speed to our destination, which in this case was the hotel hosting our ten-year high school reunion.

I'd promised Corey we'd have fun, and I'd meant it. We hadn't made it to our five-year, but it was just as well. Five years ago we were still living at home and working part-time. Corey had just graduated college with a business degree he wasn't using, and I was spending every cent I made buying and restoring old motorcycles. Sometimes I made a few bucks, and sometimes—most of the time, if I was being honest—my pastime had been more a labor of love than anything that might have turned into a career.

It wasn't until we put our minds together and decided to open a custom bike shop about forty minutes outside Boston with a buddy of ours that our lives really began.

Stepping through the door to the hotel ballroom where our reunion was being held, I scanned the room for familiar faces. Whether it was to find ones I wanted to avoid or ones I wanted to talk to, I wasn't actually sure. When we didn't recognize anyone right away, we headed to the bar. "What are we drinking tonight?" I asked Corey.

"We *are* at our high school reunion, so let's throw it back to 2006."

"You're going to tell Ava Blaine you've loved her since the second grade and then pass out on the hood of Dad's Sentra?"

Corey's eyes grew serious, like they were lost in the memory of that ridiculous moment. "That was a bad night. I didn't drink for a full year after that," he said with a shake of his head. He put his hands on the bar and called to the bartender, "Two Captain and Cokes, please."

"Ahh," I said, tossing some money onto the bar after we got our drinks. "I forgot about your Captain phase."

"Me too," Corey said. "I don't think I've even had one in almost a decade. They were my go-to for most of junior and senior year, though." He craned his neck and scanned the room. "You think Ava's here? I heard she's divorced now."

"Where'd you hear that?"

I looked at him, but he avoided eye contact. "Facebook."

"Seriously? You're such a stalker." I laughed. "If you plan to talk to her, you should probably make sure it happens before your seventh drink this time."

"You're a wise man, Colton," Corey said with a smile before taking a sip.

I shrugged. "Well, I *am* your older brother." I loved making this distinction, but the truth was, Corey and I shared everything. We always had. From our birthday to our group of friends to our clothes and cars. Growing up, nothing belonged to only one of us.

Well, everything except girls. That was a line we would never cross. If one of us was into someone—or especially if one of us had hooked up with someone—she was off-limits to the other brother. Forever. That rule limited Corey's selection of females greatly when we were in high school, but I couldn't be blamed for taking opportunities as they arose just because it made his potential dating pool smaller.

We talked at the bar for a few more minutes until we spotted a few of our old lacrosse teammates sitting at a table with their wives. We hadn't seen any of them in person in at least seven years, and time didn't appear to have been kind to them. Josh Graham and Scottie Gibson sat, their hands toying with beers they absentmindedly brought to their lips every so often, as their wives chatted. The guys didn't look thrilled, but they didn't exactly look annoyed either. Just...spacey.

"CJ!" they yelled as we approached the table, greeting us with the name everyone used in high school. It was easier for people to just use our first and last initials—which were the same—than to tell us apart. I'm not sure what they would've done if we'd had different first initials.

We spent a half hour or so catching up with Josh and Scottie who, it turned out, both had infants at home. Tonight was their first real night out since their kids had been born, and they were exhausted. It had been their wives, Marissa and Sophia, who had really wanted to come, since they were both graduates of our school as well. They didn't look familiar to me, and their names didn't ring a bell either. Which hopefully meant I hadn't messed around with them in high school.

"I'm already dreading getting up in the middle of the night," Scottie said. "Nicholas wakes up every three hours."

"You act like you're the one who has to get up to feed him," Sophia joked. "I know you gained a few sympathy pounds, but I'm pretty sure your breasts still can't feed a newborn."

They all laughed until Josh explained that Marissa

pumped as well as nursed, and in order for Josh to bond with their daughter, Marissa had gotten him some sort of bra that held bottles so the baby could "nurse" from him as well. The table got eerily quiet, and I realized what had most likely caused Josh's gray hairs.

"You're a good mom, Josh," I said.

"And you're an asshole, CJ," Josh countered with a laugh. "What's up with you guys?"

"Well, I'm not breastfeeding," I answered. "So nothing too exciting. We live in the suburbs now."

Corey added, "We opened a custom motorcycle shop with a buddy of ours a few years ago in Canton."

Scottie and Josh looked simultaneously heartbroken and envious. "Oh wow," Scottie said.

"They build bikes," Josh added sadly.

Marissa rolled her eyes at Scottie and her husband. "You two are pathetic."

"Thank you," Josh said. "That's what we're saying."

"That's awesome, though," Scottie said. "I'm happy for you guys. You seem happy, and you're both in great shape. Don't ever get married and have kids. It sucks the life out of you."

I didn't disagree. Why Corey longed for that life—one that would most likely ruin the one he had—made absolutely no sense to me. I would much rather live life as it comes instead of getting attached to something that most likely wouldn't last.

"Well, as much as I love talking about male breastfeeding, I'm gonna have to excuse myself for a few minutes. Anyone want another drink?" I stood, waiting to see if anyone wanted to take me up on my offer, but no one did.

"Captain and Coke, right?" the bartender asked, probably

remembering me because there had been two of us when we'd ordered.

I nodded.

Instead of heading straight back to the table of desperate housewives—and I wasn't talking about the women—I decided to hang out at the bar for a bit. It would be a good vantage point to see the rest of the room, and I could skim the event page on my phone to see who was even here.

All these people looked so different from what I remembered...and from their profile pictures, which all seemed to be taken from a height that indicated the photographer was a drone and not an actual person.

I couldn't help but feel a little out of place, and the realization surprised me. I looked back at Josh and Scottie's table and saw Corey talking to them and laughing with another woman who looked completely unfamiliar to me. Maybe I was getting early Alzheimer's. For some reason, it had seemed important to go to this thing, to show everyone I actually made something of myself. Though I wouldn't have admitted it at the time, I hadn't been anything to idolize in high school. I had been an okay athlete with an even less okay GPA.

I was busy scrolling through the reunion event page when a woman a few seats down the bar said, "You look like you're having about as much fun as I am."

I smiled at her and gave a wave as I mentally flipped through our graduating class in my head. But for the life of me, I couldn't think of anyone who looked like this woman—shiny blond hair that stopped at her chin in a trendy asymmetrical cut and eyes so blue it was like looking at the sky on a summer day.

"Yeah." I laughed to myself about how I must look, sitting

at the bar alone on my phone instead of catching up with people I hadn't seen in ages. "Guess I thought more of my old friends would be here. I'm blaming their absence on the fact that this thing was held on the night before Thanksgiving. Who the hell planned this?"

"I'm assuming our class president. But I can't quite remember who that is."

When she stopped talking, I realized I'd been nodding absently as she spoke. She was beautiful. *Who is this woman?*

"Gotcha," I said, ceasing the awkward movement of my head. "What about you?" I asked, hoping to buy myself some time before she realized I had no clue who she was. "Did you see many of your friends?"

She brought her hand up to tuck her hair behind one ear, even though it was already there. "A few." Her gaze dropped to the stem of her wineglass, and she spun it back and forth between her fingers like she was deciding whether she should say what she was thinking. She opened her mouth but then closed it quickly.

"What? What is it?"

"It's going to sound stupid," she said, closing the small gap at the bar between us. "But seeing you actually made a dull night a little better. I was hoping you'd be here, but I didn't see you post in the group, and you were only a 'maybe' to attend. Are you here with anyone?"

"Just my better half," I joked, though the statement held more truth than she probably realized.

Her smile, which had been beaming only seconds ago, faded. "Oh." I didn't miss her glance at my hand. "So are you engaged, or..."

"Engaged?" I asked, confused. "No, I'm not engaged."

13

"So she's your girlfriend, then?"

Suddenly realizing where her confusion must have come from, I quickly corrected her. "I'm not here with a fiancée or a girlfriend. When I said my better half, I meant my brother."

"Of course," she said, her voice sounding relieved. "I shouldn't be surprised. The only time I remember you being apart is when you had separate classes." She laughed, looking embarrassed, but she wasn't the one who should have been feeling that way, when I still had no clue who she was. "That's nice of you to say he's the better half." She took a sip of wine and scanned the room for a moment. "Though I'd have to disagree. I always liked you much better."

I felt my eyes light up at her comment. "Really?" Why couldn't I figure out who this woman was?

"Yeah," she said, shrugging. "Sorry. I know he's your brother, but he always kind of annoyed me. You look alike, but your personalities couldn't be more different. You're still CJ, since that's the only name anyone called either of you, but I always knew who was who."

"That's impressive. Even our friends couldn't tell who was who half the time." *And it's even more impressive because I have no idea who you are.* "And that's fine about the name. Being called CJ reminds me of home. I like it. So are *you* here with anyone? Fiancée? Girlfriend?"

She laughed. "No girlfriend. I'm straight. I'm as boring as I was in high school."

"I don't remember you being boring." *I don't remember you at all. God, please tell me your name. Please.*

"You're still sweet, I see."

I wasn't sure what would make her say that, because there weren't many members of the opposite sex that would've referred to me as a sweet teenager. I'd used charisma and popularity to boost an ego I shouldn't have ever had. "Thanks," I said, not really sure of an appropriate reply.

"You're just as cute as you were back then too. Cuter actually. You look like you've bulked up a little," she said with a flush of her cheeks. We were both quiet for a few moments before she continued. "Sorry. I don't really speak this directly to men I'm attracted to, but I feel like since we know each other already, it's not as weird." Her face grew even redder. "Or maybe it's weirder. I don't know."

Her comment, combined with the way she bit her lip as she looked at me, made my cock jump in my pants. I cleared my throat and tried not to stare directly at her breasts when my gaze dropped a bit. "I work out." *God, I sound like such a tool.* I might as well have said, *I pick things up and I put them down* in my best Arnold accent.

"I can tell," she said softly. She put a hand on my bicep and squeezed. "These look dangerous."

"And you look..." This time I couldn't help but take all of her in. I ran my gaze down the length of her—a petite frame with curves in all the right places, tits that would fit perfectly in my hands, a navy dress that brought out her eyes and clung to her ivory skin. "You look amazing. Like really amazing. God, I'm really great with words tonight, aren't I?" I said with a laugh.

"You're fine. That's nice of you to say. You have no idea who I am, do you?"

Shit. Embarrassed, I brought my hand to my forehead. "I don't. I'm so sorry."

She laughed, and then I did too. Despite my humiliation, I felt at ease knowing it wasn't a big deal that I didn't recognize her.

"Are you going to tell me, or are you going to make me guess?"

She smiled, and I couldn't take my eyes off her lips—shiny and wet with whatever gloss she had on them. I wondered what it might taste like. "Zara Pierce."

I thought back to the girl in braces who'd had a locker across the hall from mine...the one who'd constantly had her books all over the floor between classes...the one who'd worn scrunchies and gave teachers handmade gifts as a sixteen-year-old. It was nearly impossible to believe the woman sitting next to me was the same human being.

"No shit. Last time I saw you, you were..." I left my sentence unfinished because I couldn't think of anything to say that wouldn't come out the wrong way.

"Performing a one-woman monologue on feminism for the talent show?" She covered her eyes and then lifted her hand to peek at me.

The memory made her blush even more, and I knew why. Zara and I hadn't run in the same circles. Mine had revolved around parties and motorcycles, while hers had focused more on woodwind instruments and Hi-Q competitions. I'd always felt like she'd looked down on me a bit, but it wasn't like I'd had any desire to hang out with her either.

"I was gonna say a brunette."

ZARA

CJ and I talked for at least forty-five minutes—mostly about unimportant topics like the bartender's resemblance to Neil Patrick Harris and the horrendous choice in music that we presumed was also chosen by our class president, whose name we finally figured out after some cyber-research.

Looking into those dark-green eyes that stared back into mine, I silently thanked myself for not leaving earlier when I'd spilled red wine on my dress. It wasn't that people could necessarily see it—the dress was dark and so was the room— but I've always been someone who believed in subtle signs. Like an umbrella not opening right when it begins to rain or charcoal toothpaste leaving black marks on my teeth before a date. They were the universe's signals to me that I should stop what I'm doing and turn back or not even leave my house to begin with. That it was time to retreat because the mission was compromised.

Abort, abort, my brain had screamed after my wine spill. Tomorrow was another day, and I could try again. Or not, because my ten-year high school reunion only happened once, and there was no way my friends would have let me ditch them.

Truthfully, this whole reunion thing wasn't exactly my scene, but Becca and Trinity had begged me to go. In high school, it had always been the three of us, and they said the thought of attending an event like this without me would be akin to TLC performing after Left Eye's accident. I'd pointed out that they *did,* in fact, perform again after the singer's death, but my friends weren't having it. I wasn't sure my absence would've had quite the same effect, but nonetheless, I acquiesced. And I was glad I did.

"You remember Mr. Simpkiss, right?"

He thought for a few seconds. "The physics teacher?"

I nodded, smiling. "Did you hear why he left the year after we graduated?"

"No. I didn't know he left at all." CJ seemed interested, his head resting on his palm as he leaned casually on the bar, waiting for me to continue.

"Yup. He got Mindy Tatum pregnant." I expected his eyes to go wide and his jaw to drop, but he looked confused more than anything.

"I'm not sure I know a Mindy..."

"You don't remember Mindy? She was in Mr. Simpkiss's class with us senior year." Still nothing. "She had to use that emergency shower thing because her lab partner combined the wrong chemicals or something one day."

"I must've been absent that day," he said, his expression falling like he was sad he'd missed it. I'd have sworn he was there, but it was impossible to be sure about something that happened a decade ago.

"Well, anyway, Mindy posted a picture of her ultrasound during her first semester of college and tagged Mr. Simpkiss in it. Turns out they'd been"—a shiver ran down my body with the thought of the divorced forty-year-old—"dating since right after graduation."

There was the openmouthed stare I'd been hoping for. "No shit. That's crazy. I didn't think Simpkiss had it in him." He paused for a second. "Wait, do you think he was...they were... Did he get fired because something happened *before* Mindy graduated? That's so messed up."

I shrugged. A part of me felt guilty that I was using Mindy's story as entertainment, but CJ seemed interested, so I continued. "The heart wants what the heart wants, I guess."

"I guess."

I laughed, but it was more out of embarrassment than humor. "I'm horrible at small talk."

"Everyone's that way sometimes." Whether it was because of the overhead lights or because I wanted them to, his eyes twinkled when he smiled.

"Not you," I said, my voice more serious than it had been. "You could always talk to anyone. You're naturally friendly."

He was quiet as he ran his fingers over the condensation of his glass. "I try," he said. "But sometimes it's just good acting."

"Are you acting now?"

His mouth parted, but he didn't speak right away. Instead, the left side of his lip quirked up in that way that made me imagine what it would be like to kiss it.

"No," he said softly. "I'm enjoying talking to you."

"Me too."

"Do you want to go somewhere that's a little quieter to talk?" he asked.

"I actually think I've had enough talking," I said. And then I did something I never would've had the guts to do last time we saw each other.

I leaned in to kiss him. I didn't worry if he'd pull away or if he'd tell me it was nice or that he didn't like me like that or any of the other million reasons I'd used to talk myself out of this in high school. For once, I listened to the beating in my chest that told me just to do it. Make the first move. Be fearless.

His lips touched mine, and I knew it was well worth the risk.

CHAPTER TWO

ZARA

I'd been thinking about this ever since I saw CJ sit down at the bar. The slow but needy grind of our lips against each other's. And as our tongues tangled, I was thankful I'd grown more confident over the years. I didn't even stifle the moan that found its way from my throat to his mouth, and when the vibration of it thrummed between us, he reached a hand around to the back of my neck to deepen our kiss.

My entire body tingled with sensation, like he'd somehow hit every nerve ending with that subtle touch. It had been...well, let's just say it had been a while since a man—especially one as desirable as *this* man—had kissed me like this. Every sweep of his tongue across mine and every soft nip of his teeth on my lip had me forgetting, or simply not caring, that we were behaving like this in public. And if I was being honest with myself, the idea turned me on even more.

But there were things I wanted him to do to me—and things I wanted to do to him—that were definitely not appropriate for public display. The thoughts had me pulling away, breathless. "Would you like to come up to my room? Sorry, is that too forward? Or..." *God, I sound like a hussy.* "I swear I don't make out with men at bars like this all the time. Or ever," I corrected. "But I've had a crush on you since high school, and—"

"So you said." He smiled wide, as if hearing the comment a second time excited him as much as the kiss. And based on the frustrated groan he'd released when I'd pulled away, I'd have guessed he was pretty excited. "Just for the record, I'm not complaining," he added before closing the small distance between our lips again so he could part them with his tongue. He tasted sweet, like rum and mint and something spicy I couldn't identify. "We don't have to go upstairs if you're uncomfortable with it," he whispered against my lips.

"I want to" was the only reply I could find. My attraction to him was even stronger tonight than the girlish crush I'd had on him years ago. Maybe it was something about seeing him all grown up. The long stubble on his jawline that looked like it might grow into a full beard before the night was over. It had me wondering what it might feel like between my legs. *God help me.* Or it might have been his casual confidence and how easily we'd talked. Whatever it was about this man, I wanted him.

"Just know you have my word that I'm not going to tell the guys in the locker room after practice about whatever happens between us. This isn't high school, Zara. We're two consenting adults. Two consenting, very turned-on adults. Speaking for myself at least." He cleared his throat and shifted on the bar stool, drawing my attention to the bulge in his perfectly fitted dark jeans.

"That applies to me too," I said, feeling the blush spread across my cheeks. What had gotten into me? "So before I go back to the old Zara and let my inhibitions dictate my actions, I'd like to formally invite you back to my hotel room, Mr. Jensen."

His smile broadened into a ridiculous grin. "In that case,

I'd like to accept, Ms. Pierce."

And with that, I grabbed my bag, downed the last of my Cabernet, and headed toward the elevators.

Once inside, our hands were everywhere. Mine slipping down his back to squeeze his muscular ass. His sliding up the outside of my thigh. And as his cock rubbed against my lower stomach, I wondered if we'd even make it to my room before I had him undressed. His chest was firm against mine. I wanted to feel every part of him at once—his lips on my nipples and between my thighs, his cock spreading me wide.

"God, you're sexy," he said against my collarbone. "Makes me so hard."

I wanted to tell him that he was sexy too. That I was so fucking wet already, he could use my thong as a Slip 'N Slide if he wanted to. But all that came out of my mouth was something completely unintelligible that manifested itself as an unsteady moan.

We broke contact just long enough to exit the elevator and make our way down the short hallway. I fumbled with the key card, playfully swatting his hand away from its place on my hip as he stood behind me, his rock-hard cock pressing against my ass. "If you keep that up, I'll never get this thing open."

He laughed softly, reaching around to place his hand on mine to steady it enough to key us in. Once we were both inside, he spun me against the door, pinning my hands over my head with one of his. I loved when guys took control like this, letting me feel instead of think. And all I wanted to do was feel. Feel his fingers and tongue inside me, feel how thick and hard his cock was in my hand before I felt it fill me.

"What do you want?" he asked. He waited for the answer like it would not only turn him on, but also so he could ensure he wasn't doing more than I was comfortable with.

"Your mouth," I whispered.

He released my hands. "Like this?" he asked, and I gripped his hair in pleasure as he made his way to the exposed part of my chest right above my dress.

"Lower."

He reached around to undo the clasp at the top and dragged the zipper down slowly. But he didn't let it drop. Pulling the fabric over my shoulder enough to gain access to my breasts, he brought his mouth to them, giving each of them his undivided attention. "How about now?" he asked, working his tongue over my nipple softly before giving it a tug with his teeth.

"Getting warmer," I said.

"I was hoping for hot," he teased.

"Oh, this is definitely hot."

He let go of my dress and allowed it to fall to the floor at my feet. "Not as hot as this though," he said, sliding his hand over my exposed torso as he admired it. He quirked his head to the side like he was deciding what to do with me. After a few moments that only increased the tension, he lowered himself to his knees.

He pressed his mouth to the lace fabric of my underwear until it was thoroughly soaked with his saliva and my desire for him. "You won't be needing these," he said, slipping them down my thighs and pulling them off my legs. He took a moment to kiss the inside of my ankle before working his way up the inside of my legs. I was practically writhing when he finally slid one finger inside me.

It wasn't enough. It didn't make me feel nearly full enough, and the friction was lacking because of how wet I was for him.

His finger was a tease, but his tongue—God, his tongue—was better than any I'd ever felt. And as he sucked on my clit before flicking it with the tip of his tongue, I knew I wasn't going to last long.

My legs shook with my need to come, and I moved a hand over him everywhere I could reach—his hair, his neck, his shoulders—to show him how good this felt. He seemed to be enjoying it as much as I was, like going down on me was satisfying a hunger in both of us.

"I'm gonna come," I practically yelled, searching with my other hand to grab on to something but finding nothing but the wall beside me.

It wasn't long before I couldn't hang on any longer, and my orgasm ripped through me, making my entire body pulse with its waves. "Oh my God! Jesus, Corey! So fucking good."

COLTON

Nope. This was so fucking bad.

There was no way I could stick around after a mistake like this. Not that hooking up with Zara had been a mistake. It wasn't *my* mistake, anyway. I'd enjoyed every second of it, though she'd definitely enjoyed it more than me. I'd been so fucking hard, aching with the need to come, but as Corey's name left her mouth, my erection left too. I needed to get the fuck out of here.

But I couldn't just bolt. I would look like a complete asshole. Or, more accurately, *Corey* would look like a complete asshole. Though maybe he'd look generous and giving, unselfish. Like the Mother Teresa of orgasms. I was going to make Corey look like an orgasm saint. He'd owe me big for this one.

I rose slowly up Zara's body and thought about how it would be the last time I'd get to witness the sight. Against my better judgment, I kissed her along the way. "I should probably get going," I said.

She laughed softly and buried her mouth against me. "You have a curfew?"

I tried to smile but failed. "Nah. I just... I don't feel right about asking you to reciprocate."

"Who said anything about you asking?"

My dick twitched, growing slightly but not becoming fully erect. "I'm serious. You don't need to do anything to me."

"How about if I do something *with* you?"

Fuuuuck. And now my hard-on had fully reappeared, lengthening when she grabbed ahold of it. I swallowed hard before clearing my throat, a raspy breath escaping from me as I prepared to speak. "I'll be fine. It was satisfying enough to please you." I felt like a lawyer giving his closing argument to a box full of doubtful jurors he wasn't sure would believe a word he was saying because no bigger lie had ever been told. I was the opposite of satisfied, in every way possible.

It was a toss-up between what I'd do once I got back to our dad's house. Jerk off? Or cry into my pillow because an attractive, engaging woman only took me back to her room because she thought I was my brother?

Maybe I'd do both.

CHAPTER THREE

COLTON

Stumbling down the stairs of my dad's house the next morning, bleary-eyed and stomach growling, I wondered how many times I'd descended these steps in the same condition. Though this time I wasn't so much hungover as exhausted. Last night had been...weird. Really fucking weird. And while I wasn't necessarily happy with how I'd left things with Zara, I'd left them all the same, and that was the end of it.

As I walked into the kitchen, my gaze landed on Corey sitting at the island, spooning globs of cereal into his mouth. When he caught sight of me, he arched an eyebrow and smirked.

"Where's Dad?" I asked before he could get a word out.

He set down his spoon and leaned back in the stool. "Now, now, don't try changing the subject."

"What subject? We weren't talking about anything." I rummaged around in the fridge, looking for something I felt like eating.

"What time did you get home last night, young man?"

Yanking a loaf of bread and some butter out of the refrigerator, I went about making toast, resolutely ignoring my brother.

But he wasn't to be deterred. Appearing beside me, he

hopped up on the counter and stared at me with a shit-eating grin on his face. "Last I saw, you were chatting up Zara Pierce. My, my, my, how times have changed. She used to avoid you like you'd given her a raging case of the clap."

"I was the one who avoided her," I defended. The words sounded lame even to my own ears. Truth was, until last night, I *had* thought I was the one who avoided her. But I couldn't be so sure anymore. Maybe it was a mutual disdain. One that surely wouldn't get any better if she found out who she really fooled around with after the reunion. Or during it. Whatever.

Corey clapped a hand on my shoulder. "Sure you were, Colt. Anyway, back to your disappearing act and late-night reappearance..."

He let the words hang there for me to pick up, but I stayed strong. For about fifteen seconds. A new record for me. "Okay, fine, I went back to her hotel room. Happy now?"

Corey laughed, the shit. "I am. I so am. But the question is, why aren't you?"

The next part was going to kill me to admit. He was never going to let me live it down, and if I were capable of lying to him, I would've. But he knew me too well—knew all my tells and avoidance tactics. Giving up on buttering my toast, I put everything down and gripped the counter, exhaling a deep breath before turning my head and looking at him. "She thought I was you."

I'd never seen someone's jaw drop as far as Corey's did. "Say what?"

Sighing, I turned so I was leaning against the counter. "She thought I was you."

"Stop it." His eyes widened as his smile grew. "You seriously pretended to be me to get laid? Jesus Christ, Bill

Cosby, I didn't realize you were *that* hard up."

"Like pretending to be you would ever *increase* my chances of getting laid. Get real."

"It evidently did last night," he said through a laugh.

Okay, I guess he had me there. "In my defense—"

"Oh, am I taking on your defense? Should I grab one of Dad's legal pads for notes?"

"Do you want to hear this story or not?"

He made a zipping motion over his lips and stared at me like I was Santa Claus on Christmas morning.

"So she came up to me, calling me CJ like everyone else. Then she made a big deal about how she'd always been able to tell us apart and how she'd always liked me—well *you*, I guess—but couldn't stand you, though she was really talking about me, and fuck, this is really confusing." I ran my hands over my face before pushing them through my hair. Grabbing at the longer strands on top and tugging, I tried to get last night straight in my mind. "Basically I thought she was saying she had a crush on me, but she really thought I was you the whole time, and I didn't realize it until she moaned your name while she was coming."

Corey was quiet for a moment, which was too long for him. It was starting to freak me the fuck out.

"Dude, it wasn't my fault," I practically whined. "How was I supposed to—"

"Shhh. Just stop talking."

Oh, shit. Is he actually pissed?

"You didn't have a *thing* for her or anything, did you?"

"Colton, I said shut the hell up for a second."

Normally I would've told him to go fuck himself and gone right on jabbering away, but he looked way too serious, and it was making my panic ratchet up to undiscovered levels.

He closed his eyes and then started speaking. "I'm trying to imagine what that would feel like. To be balls-deep in a beautiful woman and have her moan out my brother's name." His eyes popped open, and I could see the amusement in them. "How did you not immediately die of embarrassment? Seriously, the fact that you're still standing in front of me is a testament to how conditioned you've become to fucked-up shit happening to you. Because if that had happened to me, I'd have immediately jumped out of her window and hoped there was a bus waiting down there to finish me off."

"First off, you're a dick. And second, I didn't sleep with her. Just got her off." I turned back to my toast and took a bite. It tasted like cardboard, but eating was better than talking to my brother.

Unfortunately, it didn't stop *him* from talking to *me*. "So on a scale from one to Tom Brady choking in the Super Bowl, how embarrassed are you right now? Because I feel like you definitely just cost yourself a championship."

I walked around him to put the butter back in the fridge and withdrew a bottle of water. "I'm not embarrassed."

"Bullshit."

"I'm not. It happened and I can't change it, so there's no point in harping on it."

"Oh, I am *so* going to harp on it." He laughed as he got down from the counter.

"I hate you."

Corey waggled his eyebrows at me, but if he was going to reply, it was cut off by our dad walking in. "Morning, boys. Have a good time last night?"

I heard Corey take a deep breath to say God only knew

29

what in response, which prompted me to elbow him in the stomach and step in front of him to hide his reaction. "It was fine. Good seeing everyone again," I said.

"That's nice. Stayed out of trouble?"

"Of course," I replied quickly.

"Some of us more successfully than others," Corey mumbled, blocking the next elbow I aimed his way.

My dad either didn't hear him or chose to ignore him. "You guys ready to help me start cooking?"

"Yup," we both replied as we moved to start clearing the counters. This was our tradition. Ever since Mom died when we were fifteen, the three of us had done our damnedest to create a Thanksgiving meal she'd be proud of. It had been her favorite holiday—a day she said was just for enjoying your family without any other agenda—and we wanted to do it justice.

In the thirteen years she'd been gone, we'd gotten this down to a synchronized routine, but the timing always felt slightly off anyway. Like we were a relay team without an anchor to run the final stretch. But we ran anyway. How could we not? Sometimes it wasn't about winning. Sometimes it was about finding the strength to finish the race.

CHAPTER FOUR

ZARA

My parents' house was only fifteen minutes away from the hotel, and I dreaded every passing second. Normally I was more awake and had time to prepare myself to deal with my family, but with the whirlwind of the reunion, I felt woefully unprepared. There was never really a time when I looked forward to spending a prolonged chunk of time around my family, but holidays were by far the craziest.

There would be a beautiful meal waiting, made solely by my mother, who stayed up half the night preparing it, while my father would scrutinize whatever football game happened to be on before leading grace and carving the turkey as if both of those activities were more vital than the actual cooking that had taken place.

My sister would gush about her three daughters, who would be in matching outfits so pristine, I wondered if she locked them in glass before bringing them over. My brother-in-law, Devon, would be mostly silent, nodding along so as to appear engaged. It was like the Cleavers met the Stepford Wives. Adding me into the mix gave the evening its sole flaw— like spending hours choosing the perfect arrangement of flowers for a date only to realize there was a wilted one hiding in the middle once you'd handed them over.

I didn't know if it was always that way or if my memory was biased. But for as long as I could remember, I'd felt like I didn't quite *fit* with my family. I was too shy, too introverted, too disinterested in all the girly things my mom and sister enjoyed. So it became easier to exclude me than to drag me along. Or maybe it was just easier for *me* to exclude *myself.*

But today I had better things to fixate on: last night with CJ. The crush I'd had on him through high school had slammed back into me as full-blown lust when I'd seen him at the reunion. Where his brother, Colton, had been obnoxious and insufferable, Corey had been funny and charming. And he was still both those things.

It had gotten a little awkward right before he left, but that was probably because he wasn't sure how I'd react to him not staying the night. Something he really needn't have worried about. I wasn't a prude—casual sex was something I could engage in without getting clingy. But reciprocating his... generosity wouldn't have been a hardship. Quite the opposite. I would've liked to have had my hands, and mouth, all over him.

I pulled into my parents' driveway, which killed whatever fantasies I was having of licking CJ like a melting popsicle. For now at least. Later, when I was back home, I was sure I'd revisit them.

I got out of my car, shut my door, and popped the trunk to grab the pies I'd picked up. Not that I'd ordered any of them. My mother would never entrust me to pick out anything for our meal. I carried the three pies and a platter of cookies—my own contribution—along with my purse and tried to not drop everything as I trudged up the three steps that led to our front door. I kicked it with the toe of my knee-high boot and waited for someone to open it, hoping that happened before I dropped everything.

The door flew open, and my mom stood there with one hand on her hip. "Did you have to bang on the door like that? We have a doorbell."

Hello to you too. "My hands are full. And last time I was here, it didn't work. Did Dad fix it yet?"

Sighing heavily, she backed up so I could pass. "No. He can barely put his shoes on the right feet. You know that. *I* fixed the doorbell myself."

"Really? How'd you know how to do that?"

"You know, you really should have more faith in me, honey."

"You YouTubed it, didn't you?"

She nodded and scooted around me to hustle back to the kitchen. "You say 'YouTubed' like it's a dirty word," she called over her shoulder.

"Sorry," I said, putting the desserts on the counter. "I'm proud of you. Not a chance I would ever mess with anything electrical."

"Well, I turned off the power to the house first. Dad barely survived the half hour without *Diners, Drive-Ins, and Dives.*"

I rolled my eyes good-naturedly and noticed my mom do the same. When we caught each other, we both began laughing.

"What's that?" my mother asked when she noticed the extra bakery box.

"Cookies."

"I didn't ask you to get cookies."

I resisted the urge to roll my eyes at her, and I mentally praised myself because she definitely would have called me out on that one. "Sorry. I didn't know I needed permission to do something nice."

She put down the spoon she'd been holding and crossed her arms. "Why do you always make things a bigger deal than they need to be?"

I laughed, though I didn't find the accusation at all amusing. "Me? You're the one giving me a hard time about bringing cookies to Thanksgiving."

"I wasn't giving you a hard time. I just said I didn't ask you to get them."

"I know you didn't. Sometimes I make my own decisions," I said, my tone much too serious for a conversation about cookies. Maybe my mom was right.

She snorted, but I wasn't sure if it was because she found my comment funny or if she was scoffing at the thought of me making my own decisions. Sure, my mom and dad hadn't been supportive of my decision to get bachelor's and graduate degrees in hospitality while taking culinary classes, but the choice to go down that road had led me to financial independence. So yeah, my decisions had been pretty solid, even if she never gave me credit for them. Okay, so maybe I did make a big deal out of little things, but this was about more than just cookies.

Mom called for my sister, Brielle, who came rushing in like the kiss-ass she was.

"Oh. Hey, Zara. What do you need, Mom?"

"Can you check on the turkey for me?"

I wanted to ask why she didn't want the trained chef already in the room to check it, but I knew the answer—she was done with our conversation and effectively done with me. So I left them to it and went into the family room. Brielle's daughters were having a tea party with dolls as my dad and brother-in-law griped at the football game. Well, my dad griped. Devon more grumbled nonsense when my father did.

"Hi, Dad," I said as I leaned down to kiss his cheek.

"There's my girl," he replied, taking his eyes off the game to pull me in for a bear hug.

I turned toward the couch. "How have you been, Devon?"

"Fine, fine, just fine," he said. Repeating everything three times was a weird idiosyncrasy of his. I once asked my sister if he had OCD or something, and she nearly detached my head from my neck. I took her reaction as a yes.

I walked over to the girls and squatted down. "Can I play?"

"Did you bring a doll?" Harper, the older one, asked. There was no sarcasm or harshness to her words. Just genuine curiosity.

"Unfortunately I did not."

Her little sister Rumi looked sad at this news. "We don't have an extra one for you to play with."

"Sorry, Aunt Zara," Harper added before they both continued playing.

I stood around awkwardly before making my way back into the kitchen and asking my mom if she needed help. But a dark ball of fur darted in front of me on the way. "Oh my God!" I yelped, jumping back. "What the hell was that?"

"What?" Dad called.

"There was like a gigantic rat or something." I was already standing on the chair in the corner of the room.

"You better get down from there before Mom sees you with your feet on the furniture," he scolded. "It wasn't a rat. That's Cecil, my kitten."

"You didn't tell me you got a cat," I said, stepping down from the chair.

"I got a cat."

"I always thought Mom was allergic."

"I am!" my mom yelled in from the kitchen.

"She's not," my dad said. "And it's about time I got some testosterone in this house. Years with three women is enough to put someone in the nuthouse."

"He's so dramatic," my mom called.

"You can call me dramatic when you stop fake sneezing at the sight of Cecil."

"I don't want a black cat in here. It's a bad omen."

My dad groaned like he'd heard this argument before. He probably had. "It's only bad if it crosses your path."

I was tempted to say it just crossed *my* path, but I chose not to think about my potential bad luck. Maybe if I didn't acknowledge it verbally, the universe would forget it happened. Instead I chose to change the subject. "You need any help, Mom?"

"No, I think I'm okay."

Having checked the turkey and finding things progressing satisfactorily, my sister moved toward me and slid onto a stool at the island, where I joined her.

"How was the reunion?"

Mind-blowingly orgasmic. "Fine."

"See anyone interesting?"

She was really trying to sniff out some gossip, but since the best rumor to come out of last night involved me, I wasn't going to give her an inch. "Nope."

"I saw Maddie Gilbertson the other day. She's pregnant. Again. I wonder who the father of this one is."

The derision in her words made my shoulders tense. Maddie had had a tough life, growing up with an alcoholic father in a trailer and rumors swirling about what had gone on inside. But I'd never heard her utter an unkind word about anyone. Which was a hell of a lot more than I could say about my sister. "Wasn't she working at the bank?"

"Yeah. So?"

"So she has a solid-paying job that she's managed to hold on to since we graduated high school. That says a lot about her character."

Brielle snorted. "So does having three kids by three different men. And she's probably off with someone else as we speak."

"You want to know what she's probably *not* doing?"

"What?" my sister asked, leaning in excitedly.

I shifted closer to her, like I had a salacious secret to share. "Talking shit about you over Thanksgiving dinner."

Brielle reared back, glaring at me before sliding off her stool and leaving the room.

"Can't you try to get along with Brielle so we can have a nice meal together?" my mom asked, clearly exasperated.

"Not when doing so requires me to be an asshole."

"Such language." All that was missing was the *tsk*.

We were silent after that. Even when she called everyone to dinner and we began eating, quiet prevailed. That was the problem when not one of us had a single thing in common with any other member of our family. We had fuck-all to talk about unless we were bickering about nonsense. Maybe that's why we resorted to it so often. It brought us closer together while we pushed each other apart.

I briefly thought about telling them about my new business venture, but I really didn't need to hear any negative comments about it. Not that they would've really cared anyway. It would've been a painful two-minute blip in an already strange evening.

Once dessert was over—during which my mom didn't even bother to put out the cookies I'd brought—I couldn't get out of there fast enough. I grabbed my cookie tray, said quick goodbyes, and practically sprinted to my car.

I let myself unwind for a second before turning the ignition and making the half-hour drive home. With as mentally exhausted as I was, part of me wished I'd booked another night at the hotel, but I knew I'd feel better in my own bed. When I pulled up to my town house, I dragged my things inside and took them to my bedroom. A bath sounded wonderful. I'd basically thrown everything into my bag that morning, so I had to sift through its contents to find my toiletries and put everything into piles: laundry, toiletries, jewelry...

I pulled the thong I'd worn last night out of my bag, and a shiny object came with it before falling to the floor. I picked it up and studied it. The gold chain in my hand held a beautiful pendant. It definitely wasn't mine, which left only one person it could belong to.

My heart rate spiked at the thought, and an arousing throb pulsed in my clit. This gave me an excuse to see CJ again. There was no way I was going to suggest mailing it to him. I might not have time for a boyfriend, but getting fucked into the mattress by my high school crush? *That* I had time for.

CHAPTER FIVE

COLTON

My phone dinged, but I was too frantic to check it. I couldn't find my mom's necklace anywhere. It wasn't until halfway through the day that I'd realized it was missing because I took for granted it was where it always was: wrapped safely around my neck. I never took it off. Ever. So when I reached up to clasp it as we said grace before dinner, I nearly had a panic attack when my hand touched nothing but my own chest.

Where the fuck could it be?

Okay, I had to calm down. *Way* down. I had already ripped my childhood bedroom apart and turned up nothing. I needed to be more methodical in my approach. Where had I last had it?

"Dude, what the fuck?" Corey's voice from the doorway sounded alarmed.

Sinking onto the bed, I dropped my head into my hands. "I lost it, Cor. I fucking lost it."

Barely a second passed before I felt the bed dip beside me and a hand roughly squeeze the back of my neck. "We'll find it." He knew exactly what I was referring to. Of course he did. There was only one thing that would cause this kind of reaction in me, and no one knew me better than him. "I'll check the bathroom." He was out of the room before I could tell him I'd already looked there, but it was probably best to have him double-check anyway.

When he returned with tense shoulders, I knew he hadn't found it. He began digging around the mess I'd made of the room, and I did the same.

"Where did you have it last?"

Despite having just asked myself the same question, I was irritated by him asking it. "If I knew that, I wouldn't be ransacking my room, would I?" I snapped.

He stood up and pointed at me like he was somehow threatening or intimidating or some other shit that wasn't true. We were the same size, and he hadn't been able to take me down since before puberty. "Don't start acting like a dick. I'm trying to help you."

I wanted to tell him to shove his "help" straight up his ass, but I also knew I needed it. My phone began ringing the sound of a screeching alarm—the only thing I was guaranteed to hear in the shop.

"Answer that thing, will ya?" Corey griped as he tossed a pile of clothes onto my bed. "I don't know how you stand that ringtone."

I dug around for the phone and followed the obnoxious sound until I found it beneath a stack of magazines. By the time I grabbed it, whoever had been calling had hung up. I didn't recognize the number, but there was also a text alert, so I swiped my finger across the screen and went into my messages.

The same number that had just called had sent a picture of my mom's necklace dangling from a pair of black lace panties.

*Found this attached to my
thong from last night. Yours?*

Thank Christ.

"If Mom could only see her family heirloom now. She'd be so proud," Corey said over my shoulder, startling the hell out of me.

"Shut up," I muttered as I went back into my missed call log and hit what was obviously Zara's number.

"Do you think Mom ever got that necklace stuck on her own thong? Or Grandmom perhaps?"

"You're sick, you asshole," I said just as Zara answered the phone.

"Um, what?" she said, sounding taken aback.

"Shit, sorry. Not you," I said into the phone. "I was talking to my brother."

Corey crowded close to me, even though I tried pushing him away.

"How is Colton anyway?" she asked.

Corey pulled away so he could look at me, a broad smile spreading across his face and his eyes alight with pure joy. I slapped him on the side of the head.

"He's good. I don't know where I'd be without him, actually. He's basically the only reason I have a job," I replied with a smirk of my own.

"You asshole. Give me the phone," Corey said as he tried to wrestle the phone away from me. "Lies. All lies, Zara," he yelled as we struggled. "My brother tells the *biggest* lies. You should ask him about them."

Finally managing to push him away from me, I jumped over my bed and took off for the bathroom. I slammed the door in Corey's face, locked it, and then leaned against it, trying to catch my breath.

"I'm so glad you guys have matured so much since high

school," Zara said, her voice tinged with amusement. Or at least what I hoped was amusement.

"Sorry. We don't exactly bring out the best in each other." Which wasn't strictly the truth. We goofed off something fierce, but we also pushed each other to be the best we could be. It was a double-edged sword—one side made us morons and the other made us successful. I was thankful for the balance. "So you found my necklace. I was tearing my house apart looking for it. Thank you for calling."

"Sure. Do you want me to mail it, or..."

"Or...?"

"Or I can attach it to the G-string I'm currently wearing, and you can come take it off." Her voice was raspy and seductive, and it was making my cock thicken in my sweat pants.

"The G-string or the necklace?" I asked.

"Both."

"Text me your address. I'll be right there."

ZARA

After getting off the phone with CJ, I raced through a shower and tidied up my room. I dressed in a seafoam-green bra and thong set I hadn't worn yet but stopped short of attaching the necklace to my panties like I'd told him I would. From how relieved he sounded when he heard I'd found it, it was clearly important to him. I wasn't sure dangling it over my clit would be appropriate.

I contemplated clasping it around my neck, but wearing it didn't seem right either. Instead, I nestled the delicate gold chain into the cup of my bra so that the pendant, which upon closer inspection looked like some kind of beautiful ancient coin, hung over the lace exterior. This way he'd still have to touch me to reclaim it, but it didn't feel so...dirty.

Not that dirty was a bad thing. I was hoping to get up to a lot of dirty things with CJ this evening, but I didn't want to profane something that could potentially be important to him.

My doorbell chimed, and I grabbed a robe off the bed before hurrying downstairs. Running my hands through my hair one last time, I swung the door open to reveal CJ looking hot as hell in a light-blue hoodie and gray sweat pants that did nothing to hide his bulge.

I should say something.

Instead, I stepped back from the door and motioned him inside.

He'd always been a well-built guy in high school, but he'd grown into a man whose presence took over a room. He was solid and muscled, but it wasn't the kind of physique one procured from spending hours in the gym. It was the kind of body a man got from doing...manly things. *Jesus, his hotness makes me stupid.*

He pushed up the sleeves of his hoodie, and my gaze was drawn to the movement. I wanted to map the corded muscle in his forearms with my tongue. Knowing from experience just how capable his large hands were, wetness flooded south, and my clit pulsed with anticipation.

"So you found my mom's necklace?" His voice rumbled through me, making me shiver.

I nodded. "It's beautiful."

He flexed his hands by his sides, as if he was struggling to keep them where they were. Which was the last thing I wanted. "My mom wore it all the time. I was always fascinated by it. It's an ancient Chinese gaming chip made from mother-of-pearl."

Which meant it was probably super expensive and shouldn't be dangling from my bra, but that ship had sailed.

"Can I see it?" The huskiness of his voice made me relax. He was clearly hoping it was somewhere on me.

Or maybe *I* was hoping he was hoping that. Either way, I unfastened the belt tied at my waist and pushed the robe off my shoulder, letting it fall to a heap on the floor.

His eyes drifted to my thong first, but when he didn't see the necklace, he let his gaze slowly drift up my body until he settled it on the necklace. Stepping closer, he slowly placed his hands on my shoulders.

The roughness of his hands against the softness of my shoulders felt amazing. He slid his fingertips down over my collarbone and to the swell of my breasts. Then he stopped their course and looked into my eyes. "I've never seen that necklace look more beautiful."

I don't know who moved first after that. Suddenly his lips were on mine or mine were on his, and we both moaned into the kiss as our hands explored each other greedily. The kiss was consuming, like an inferno sucking all the oxygen from us both to sustain itself. Feeling his tongue caress my lips, I instantly opened for him, letting him drag me deeper into the moment.

He pulled back slightly, and I chased his lips, too intoxicated by the taste of him to stop.

"I just," he gusted out before putting his lips back on mine where they belonged. "I... We need to talk." He managed to get the words out in between deep, probing kisses.

I gently removed the necklace and placed it in his hand before reaching back to unclasp my bra and let it slip down my arms and join my robe on the floor. "There are much better uses for your mouth than talking," I said.

He zeroed in on my hardened nipples, and he moved his hands up slowly to cup my breasts. The coolness of the coin felt amazing against the heated flush of my skin. He grazed over my nipples with his thumbs, causing me to arch toward him.

"But I really—"

"CJ."

He brought his gaze back up to my face and waited for me to continue.

"Make me come."

Bringing one hand up to my nape, he pulled me to him and kissed me hungrily. *This* was what I needed. Talking was for people who were interested in dating and getting to know each other. That wasn't what this was. This was need, pure and physical. And it seemed he was finally fully with the program.

He put the necklace into his pocket before sliding his hands over my hips and then gripped my ass, pulling me against him. His hard cock pressed into my belly, and I wanted to see it, touch it, *feel* it.

"Bedroom?" he asked.

I pointed up the steps without moving my body away from his. He looked where I'd gestured for a second before lifting me by the backs of my thighs and carrying me upstairs. Since my room was the first door at the top of the stairs, it wasn't hard for him to find, and he carried me inside, his lips still fused to mine.

Lowering me onto the bed gently, he then stepped back and tore his hoodie off, revealing bare skin beneath. When he shucked his sweat pants, his erection sprang free. CJ had come prepared, and since I was prepared to come, I was supremely thankful for his choice to not wear anything under his pants.

He moved toward me, grabbed my thong, and pulled it off me.

"I have condoms in the drawer." My voice was breathier than I'd ever heard it, and I was momentarily worried what this man might reduce me to before this night was done.

His long, thick cock bobbed as he made his way over to the drawer and opened it, removing a condom, tearing it open, and rolling it over himself. He seemed ready to pick up where we left off the previous night, skipping the foreplay neither of us needed. Crawling between my spread legs on the bed, he lowered himself so his chest touched mine.

As he kissed me deeply, his cock slid over my clit, collecting the moisture that had gathered there. I was beyond turned on, and I arched into him so my nipples rubbed against skin that was taut over firm pecs. Just as I was about to take him in hand and guide him to my entrance, he did it himself, positioning the blunt head of his cock against me and pushing steadily inside.

Gasping, I grasped hold of his back, my fingernails no doubt leaving scratches behind. He rocked into me gently at first, letting me get used to how thick he was. But as his mouth moved down to suck on the tender skin on my neck, his thrusts picked up speed and intensity.

"Yeah," I groaned. "Just like that."

Shifting so his weight was on his palms, he looked down at where we were joined and pulled almost all the way out before snapping his hips forward and driving back in. I could feel every ridge and vein on his cock as it massaged the walls of my pussy. All I could do was hold on for the ride and make unintelligible noises of encouragement.

"Fuck. Feels so good," he gritted out as he threw his head back, clearly giving himself over to sensation. But he quickly refocused on me, moving one hand down to rub my clit.

Part of me wanted to tell him to stop. My orgasm was already building low in my belly, and with the way he was working my clit, this was going to be over sooner than I wanted it to be. But the bigger part of me wanted to get off. I had a feeling the explosion was going to be nuclear, and I wanted it.

He seemed to be on the same page. "Close," he ground out before quickening his pace even more, chasing the release he hadn't let me give him the previous night.

I wanted to watch him get there. Wanted to see his face as his orgasm took him over. As his finger continued to work magic on me, my clit nearly ached with pleasure, and I couldn't hold back anymore. My body went rigid as I came, but I forced my eyes to stay open. I went pliant beneath him but still met his thrusts, even as they became more erratic.

His hips flexed as he pushed deeply into me, his cock seemingly trying to burrow inside. After a few hard, long thrusts, he groaned and dropped to his elbows, his body quaking as he no doubt flooded the condom with come. His whole body was taut above me as he rocked gently a couple more times, probably trying to milk his orgasm for all it was worth.

Eventually he came back to himself. He looked down at me and pecked a kiss to my lips before rolling to his side and getting up to deal with the condom. When he came back, I was still lying on my bed, my body content to ride the wave of satisfaction a little longer.

"Did I break you?" he asked, amusement and a trace of smug pride in his tone.

I laughed at his ridiculousness but answered honestly. "Not yet. But you're welcome to give it another try."

CHAPTER SIX

COLTON

"You guys doing anything today? I could use your help at the restaurant this morning." My dad handed me a cup of coffee before pouring one for Corey too.

"Thanks," I said, taking a sip. "And sure. What's up?" Neither one of us had worked at the restaurant since we were in high school. Even when we came back on college breaks, the place was usually staffed well enough that Dad didn't need us for anything.

"Could just use your input on some repairs I need to make. It shouldn't take long."

"No rush," Corey said. "We probably won't head home until later tonight."

Dad looked at Corey and then back to me. "I can make a tee time for tomorrow if you boys wanna stay one more night. You know... Like we used to."

The hope that lit up his eyes sent a pang of guilt through me. We used to golf every Thanksgiving weekend, starting when Corey and I were in high school. And truthfully, I missed it. But with the bike shop requiring so much of our time, the tradition had died off sometime over the last few years. "Sure, that'd be fun," I answered, and Corey echoed my sentiments.

"Great! I'll call later on." My dad's excitement was

ELIZABETH HAYLEY

audible, and he reached a hand out to squeeze my shoulder in appreciation before doing the same to Corey.

We finished our coffees, and Dad suggested we grab something to eat on the way. The fifteen-minute drive from Dad's place to the restaurant was shorter than I remembered since I'd driven it last—maybe six years ago. It reminded me of going back to our old elementary school and thinking how small the hallways had gotten since I'd left.

As a kid, the drive to the restaurant had seemed to take forever, especially after a long day at school. By the time we got to our "office," as my mom had dubbed the booth closest to the kitchen, Corey and I were ready for anything except homework. Video games, TV, bed. Just about the last thing we wanted to do was hang out in our parents' restaurant on the nights they both had to be there.

But after our mom's passing, I never entered the restaurant with the same perspective. And today was no different.

The sign still said *Maggie's*. There was just no Maggie. No dark-red hair, no sweet smile surrounded by freckles, no one to tousle my hair before giving me a kiss on the top of my head and telling me to get back to work.

The last time I'd been at Maggie's was when we threw our dad a sixtieth birthday party two years ago, and now, as I wandered around the dining room, I scolded myself for not returning sooner. For not even asking Dad if he needed any help.

Because he clearly did.

It was true the food was always the draw, not the decor or the building. But Dad had always been able to keep on top of things. But that didn't appear to be the case anymore. "What the hell happened to this place?" I asked, eyeing wallpaper

49

that was peeling off walls and a chair rail that was missing in places.

Corey ran a hand over some of the remaining wallpaper—a textured navy blue that had been on the walls since Maggie's opened twenty years ago. My mom's choice. Seeing the bare walls behind it felt wrong.

Dad shrugged. "Started some renovations last week. I figured the place could afford to be closed over the holidays."

"Can it?" I asked. The idea seemed ridiculous—irresponsible, even. This was Dad's only source of income. "How's that possible? Did you find a celebrity to blackmail or something? You have a Kardashian sex tape you're not telling us about?"

"Don't look at me," Corey said when I glanced at him for an explanation, even though I figured he wouldn't have one either. "I'm as confused as you are. When's the place supposed to reopen? This is gonna take a while. The walls are in horrible shape behind the paper. I thought you said this would take a few hours."

"Not the repairs. Those'll obviously take a long time. I just need help picking some stuff. The color blindness doesn't make this kind of thing too easy."

"Right," I said, thinking back to when Mom used to have to match his outfits for him if he wore anything other than black pants or jeans.

Dad sighed and took a seat at one of the wooden chairs at a table in the middle of the room. He looked tense, burdened. Like Corey's question was more complex than providing us with a date. It scared me. "Take a seat, boys. I need to talk to you about something."

Corey sat, slowly, across from our dad.

"I think I'd rather stand for this," I said, already sensing a gravity to the conversation.

Silence hung between all of us for a minute, making the tension thicker than a morning fog.

Finally Dad spoke. "I need your help with a few repairs here because I agreed to do some. It's not for sure yet, but the potential buyer wants to see some things done around here before they'll make a formal offer, and I haven't had any other interest."

"Potential buyer? You're selling Mom's restaurant?" I never thought this day would come. It hadn't ever crossed my mind, and my tone showed it.

"It's not Mom's restaurant anymore, Colt," my dad said. Unlike mine, his voice was quiet, somber. It was full of a sadness that was the result of more than just the mention of my mother. "It may be her namesake, but she isn't around anymore. And I just don't want to do it without her anymore."

How could I not have noticed how much Dad had begun to struggle? "We'll help you."

"Yeah." Corey reached a hand to Dad's shoulder and gave it a squeeze like Dad did so often with us when we needed consoling. "We're here now. We can be here again."

Dad nodded but didn't say anything. I wasn't sure if it was because he didn't know what to say or because he was scared of how his voice might sound when he spoke. He never liked showing any sort of weakness. I hadn't even see him cry at Mom's funeral. I'd only heard him one time after Corey and I had gone to bed and he assumed we were asleep for the night. I remember how I'd been staring at the nail pop on the ceiling above my bed for hours, willing sleep to come to me but never finding it.

Not until I heard my dad sobbing on the other side of the wall, anyway. Until that night, I'd thought crying yourself to sleep was just a saying—an exaggeration used for effect and not grounded in any sort of reality. But as the first tear rolled down my cheek and found its way to my pillow, I realized just how real the possibility was. I wasn't sure if I was crying for the loss of my mom or for my dad's loss of his wife. But the reason didn't matter. I'd woken up the next morning with my eyes puffy and red and no memory of falling asleep.

My dad looked to each of us, his eyes holding an appreciation that I knew he'd never be able to verbalize. "I can't ask you guys to do that. That's why I'm doing this. You get that?"

"What I get is that we're your family, and you need our help," Corey said before looking over to me. "Tell him, Colt."

"Cor's right. We can get this place fixed up. Couple of days, tops. You don't have to sell it if you don't want to."

Dad stood, grabbed some color swatches off one of the nearby tables, and walked over to the wall. He turned around to where we were both now standing, our faces no doubt holding the same baffled expression. "Gray or tan?" he asked. "Mom was never too fond of blue."

We spent most of the day helping at the restaurant, choosing colors for the walls, tearing down the rest of the wallpaper, ripping up the carpet that hadn't been replaced... well, ever. We'd get someone else to install a new one—we weren't delusional enough to think we could tackle that ourselves—but we figured removing the old carpet might bring the cost of the job down some. By the time we finally left, we'd actually made some decent progress.

And not just in regard to the repairs. It took a while, but

Corey and I tried our best to understand where our dad was coming from. He'd been running a restaurant on his own for years when it hadn't been meant to be his alone. Not only was it physically taxing, but the emotional strain it must've put on him wasn't one I'd ever considered before he'd explained it to us.

It was like a fucked-up version of *Groundhog Day*. No matter how much my dad hoped and prayed that things would be different—easier—when he opened the restaurant each day, it was the same shit all over again. He was struggling to add variety to a menu that had been the same for over a decade, and when the head chef left for a more upscale restaurant a year ago and Dad hadn't been able to replace him, business had slowly declined.

The realization made me feel guiltier than I cared to admit, because when it came down to it, I should've known he needed help, and I should've offered to provide it.

"You wanna move up to the ladies' tee so you have a chance to hit the green this time?"

Corey's question pulled me back to the moment—the one where it was my turn on a par three.

"There's a group behind us," Corey said, nodding toward the last hole. "You gonna play, or you gonna stare at the clouds all day?"

"I'm not staring at the clouds. I'm strategizing my next shot."

My dad laughed before turning to Corey. "Water or rough?" he teased as he gazed up at the sky. "What do you think, Cor?"

Corey chuckled, and even I couldn't help but crack a smile. Corey and my dad always busted my balls when we got together, especially when it involved golf.

"It's a tough decision," Corey said. "He could always put it in the sand too."

"I'm not gonna get it in the sand," I said, as if the possibility was a ridiculous one.

My dad walked over to the cart and put his driver back in his bag. "I don't think you will either," he called. "Bunkers are too close to the hole, and you like to stay away from there."

"I hate both of you," I said dryly. "I'm like the Tiger Woods of Massachusetts."

"Yeah, Tiger Woods without the skill or women," Corey replied with an amused smile. "Well, to be fair, you do have a woman. Kind of, anyway."

As I leaned down to put the ball on the tee, I saw my dad's eyebrows raise. "Kind of?"

Sighing, I backed away from the tee to look at him. "Corey's kidding. It's nothing." That's when it occurred to me that I'd promised Zara I wouldn't say anything to anyone but then told Corey. Maybe I *was* still the dick she remembered I was in high school.

"Oh, all right," my dad said with curiosity in his inflection that I wasn't going to indulge. "If you say so."

Then I set up and hit the ball right into the trees on the left, causing my brother and Dad to laugh hysterically.

My dad got into the driver's seat of the golf cart. "Maybe you should consider driving the ball with an actual driver."

"I like my three wood. I have more control with it."

"Sure, sure," my dad teased. "I got it. Control put that ball over in the leaves."

"Listen, old man, we have four holes left. It ain't over 'til it's over."

"I'm ten over par. You're thirty-eight, Tiger."

A few minutes later, we finished the hole, and my dad didn't miss the opportunity to tell me that I was now forty over.

"Keep bullying me, and I won't buy you the hot dog and beer I promised."

"Who the hell eats just one hot dog? You're buying me two," he said.

"You're tough."

"And you're cheap," Corey chimed in from the back seat.

I turned around to smack his leg, but he pulled away like he knew the assault was coming. "I don't see you offering to pay for anything."

"I paid for the round of golf."

Shit. "I forgot about that. Guess I'll buy you a hot dog and a beer too, then."

"You're too generous," he said, his voice flat with irony.

When we finished the round, I accepted my defeat and we headed into the clubhouse to grab a bite to eat. I handed my dad his two dogs first and then set Corey's down on the table in front of him. I dumped condiments in the center of the table and went back for the beers. "Thanks for your help," I said when I returned.

Corey shrugged. "It's my reward for putting up with you."

"What do *I* get?" Dad asked. "I've had to deal with both of you for twenty-eight years."

"He's got a point," I said before washing down the dog with some beer.

"That he does," Corey agreed. "A morning of golf with your two favorite people good enough?"

Putting down his food, our dad smiled. "It's better than good enough. The best."

CHAPTER SEVEN

ZARA

Waking up this early on a Sunday wasn't something I was used to, but after a Thanksgiving weekend, a long class at the gym was a necessity. And there was no better burn than a spin class. I tried to go to Transform at least once or twice a week to sweat out some of the calories I regularly consumed. Being in the culinary industry didn't make it easy to always eat well. And recently I'd been working on some new recipes.

After swiping my membership card at the desk, I grabbed two small towels from the nearby shelf and headed to the spin studio. I could usually claim a bike toward the back because classes in the afternoon or mornings on weekdays tended to be less crowded. But the Sunday after Thanksgiving proved differently, and I was disappointed I hadn't thought of it beforehand.

I glanced around the dim studio to see the only two free bikes were in the front row. I walked over to the one closest to the door and put my towel over the handlebars, but the person next to me spoke. "Actually, that one's my wife's." He pointed to the door. "She just went to refill her water."

I apologized and then headed to the other bike farther down, only to be told that that one had a broken pedal that hadn't been fixed yet.

"Take mine," I heard a familiar voice say, though I couldn't place it right away.

I looked toward it and saw CJ getting off a bike toward the back and already wiping it down.

"What are *you* doing here?" I asked.

He smiled. "Good morning to you too."

I probably blushed, and I was thankful the dim lights meant he probably hadn't noticed. "Sorry," I said. "Good morning." I headed over to where his bike was, but I had no intention to take it. "Seriously though. Why are you here? At this gym, I mean. You don't live near here."

"I'm not going home until later today, so I figured I'd just come to this gym instead. I'm more of a morning workout person, I guess."

"I'm not a morning person at all," I replied.

"Well, you're here now." He gestured to the bike. "All yours. Enjoy your workout." He smiled before heading for the exit.

It wasn't long before I was behind him, telling him I wasn't going to take his spot in the class. "You were here first. I'm not going to steal your workout."

"You're not stealing it if I give it to you," he said. "I've already been biking for twenty minutes, and the class would've been a warm-up anyway. I have other stuff I can be doing."

My eyes widened in what I'm sure looked like awe. Because it was. "A spin class is your *warm-up*?"

He shrugged and then ran a towel over his hair, which was slightly damp in the back. "Yeah," he said, like it was no big deal.

I could barely move after one of those classes, and this fool basically used it as an intro to...something that was no doubt much harder than riding a bike for forty-five minutes.

"You wanna work out together?" he asked.

Not particularly. Because my idea of a workout was definitely not equivalent to his. At least according to his biceps, which were clearly visible in his fitted T-shirt. The observation caused me to make other—lower—observations. Particularly below the waist. He was sporting a pair of those shorter exercise shorts that guys could only pull off if their quads were built enough. CJ was certainly one of them.

"Don't get too excited." His joke reminded me he was waiting for an answer.

"Oh. Um, yeah."

"You sure?"

"Sure I'm sure." I didn't know when it was that I got better at sex than conversation, but I was definitely more self-conscious now than when I'd been naked with this man. I gave him a smile I was hoping would reassure me as much as it did him. "You sure you can keep up with me? I'm surprisingly strong. Like a petite superhero."

He laughed. "I'll take my chances."

It wasn't clear who decided to begin with a three-mile run, though I'd like to think I wasn't to blame for that mistake. I tried not to look at his treadmill when I finally reached the three-mile mark on mine, huffing and puffing as I came to a stop.

"Okay, so maybe you're the superhero," I said, finally allowing me to eye his monitor, which showed just under four and a half miles.

"No way I'd ever wear one of those tight costumes."

I looked at him like he was a dessert I couldn't wait to get my mouth on. "Well, that's unfortunate for the rest of the population."

Letting out a loud laugh, he said, "I like to save all this for special occasions."

Now it was my turn to laugh. "Like weddings and baptisms and stuff?"

"Or class reunions. You'd be surprised how many women wanna dance with you when you're wearing a cape."

"You're a lunatic."

"You're cute."

I was sure I blushed, but I hoped he couldn't tell since I was probably still beet red from my run. He led me over to some free weights, which looked intimidating.

"I can't lift that," I said.

He set the pair of thirty-five-pound dumbbells near the mat I'd grabbed and then walked over to pick up two fifteens. "Catch," he said, pretending to toss one in my direction.

Knowing he wasn't actually going to let it leave his hand didn't stop me from flinching. "You're a gym liability." I gave him a playful shove. There was a sheen of sweat on his skin, and he smelled like salt and that masculine body wash.

And then, as if one CJ wasn't enough, another one appeared in the distance.

COLTON

Snap! My leg stung like fire from the whip of a towel. "What's up, asshole?" Corey said behind me.

I turned toward him and glared. *I will fucking kill you if you fuck with me right now.* I suddenly wished I *was* a superhero—like Cyclops, who could shoot lasers out of his eyes and eliminate someone from the earth with a single look.

"Hey," I finally managed to grit out. "I thought you were

lifting in the other part of the gym." *You better get the hell back there*, I warned with my eyes.

"Felt like some cardio." He began jogging in place and then throwing jabs in the air as he dodged an invisible opponent. What a tool. "Zara, right? My brother's told me a lot about you," he said without even bothering to stop his pretend boxing match.

She nodded and looked at him like she wished she had laser eyes too. That or a can of mace. I almost laughed, but then I realized the mace would've actually been meant for me. I needed to get him the hell out of here. And what the hell would I have told him about her other than that I slept with her? Which was exactly what I swore to her I *wouldn't* tell anyone.

This fucker had a death wish, and I'd be happy to help him achieve his dream. "Okay, well, we don't wanna hold you up. I'm sure you have a workout to get to."

"I can do some here," he said, dropping to the ground. "Check this out." He did a few normal pushups and then threw in a few claps before transitioning to some weird yoga holds.

There was no doubt about it. I would murder him in the parking lot and put his body in the dumpster.

After a few more seconds of his ridiculous show, I nudged—or more like kicked—him in the ribs. "Get moving. We're planning to exercise here."

He hopped up and gave me a squeeze on the shoulders before whispering uncomfortably in my ear, "I'll see you at home later."

Once he was on the other side of the gym and safely out of sight, I let my muscles relax a little. I hadn't even noticed how tense I'd gotten with him around. I didn't plan to keep my real identity from Zara, but the gym didn't exactly seem like a great place to come clean. And I especially didn't want it to seem like my brother and I had colluded to deceive her intentionally.

"What's wrong with him?" Zara asked, seeming almost amused by his antics.

"Must be off his meds again," I answered humorlessly. Then I picked up the heavier set of weights, and she picked up hers to follow along. I showed her a few movements—some one-leg bicep curls and tricep extensions with bands. But even though my body was engaged, my mind wasn't.

I wondered if she could tell the difference between Corey and me when we were next to each other. She'd said she could always tell us apart, and I'd believed her. Maybe once she had both of us in front of her, she'd realize her mistake. And maybe she'd never speak to me again.

But she hadn't seemed any different since Corey's departure. She was either an Oscar-worthy actress or wasn't suspicious of anything. I hoped it was the latter.

Once we finished our workout—which consisted mostly of me keeping an eye out for the natural disaster known as Hurricane Corey—I said goodbye to Zara and headed for the locker room. At least there was no chance of Zara running into both of us in there. Though there was a chance that she'd run into Corey without me. I wasn't sure which was worse. Once inside, I pulled out my phone and texted Corey to get his ass in here.

The last time another guy asked me to meet him in a locker room was when Christian Jeffrey asked if he could see my groin pull.

STFU and get in here!!!

Sigh...be there in two.

I felt every second of the hundred and twenty as I waited for him, and when he finally arrived, turning the corner without expecting me to be right there, I punched him in the stomach. I wasn't really sure why he wasn't anticipating it, but it actually made him double over, though he recovered quickly.

"What was that for?"

"For almost messing that whole thing up for me."

"What thing?"

"The thing with Zara." God, he was dense sometimes.

"Sorry," he said. The fact that he sounded genuinely apologetic made me want to hit him again, but I managed to restrain myself. "I didn't realize you had a 'thing' with her," he added, using air quotes.

"Well, it's not really a 'thing.' It's nothing really. Just having some fun. I'm gonna tell her I'm not you, but she stopped me the other day when I was about to, and today wasn't exactly the right time. You know...since you were standing right next to me."

"What do you mean? That would've been perfect. Then Zara would've realized you're the one she can't stand, and I would've been there to console her when she felt betrayed."

"You're like the worst brother ever," I said dryly, but I was sure Corey knew I was kidding.

"Well, in all fairness, I'm the only one you got, so you don't really have much to compare me to."

"I'm pretty sure I would've liked Cain better."

He laughed, and it made me laugh too. "What the fuck

were you doing with all those pushups and shit out there, by the way? You looked like an arrogant tool."

Corey pulled his head back like the question surprised him. "Wasn't it obvious? I was impersonating you."

"You asshole." I laughed again. "I don't do that shit."

"Not now you don't. But you did in high school, and that's the Colton she remembers. Come to think of it, you should actually be thanking me. There's no way she'll think *I'm* Corey when I just acted like a complete jackass."

I would never give Corey the satisfaction of knowing that I thought his point was actually valid. "I doubt it took much acting," I said. I grabbed my wallet and keys out of my locker and tossed the keys at him. "Let's go. You're driving."

CHAPTER EIGHT

COLTON

"Weren't you supposed to leave fifteen minutes ago?" Wes, one of my bike builders, asked.

I sighed and stared at the bike I was working on for a second before standing and beginning to put my tools away. "If I didn't know better, I'd think you were trying to get rid of me."

Wes laughed. "You know what they say. When the boss is away..."

"The dipshits fuck everything up and my business goes to hell?"

That only made him laugh harder. "Absolutely." Wes had been working for us for a little over six months, and I wasn't sure how we'd ever survived without him. The guy was a workhorse who was always in a good mood. At only twenty-three, the kid was a total gearhead who could build and fix anything motorcycle related. But he was also a clown.

"Jayce will be here until the end of the day in case anything comes up." There was no way we trusted Wes to close up. Not because we thought he'd steal from us or anything like that, but because the only time his ADHD was under control was when he was tinkering with a bike. The kid would end up locking himself in the bathroom or something. And even though Jayce didn't work with the bikes—he was in charge of our marketing and social media accounts—he still had more common sense about shop needs than Wes.

His smile widened into a smirk. "What would I do without my three dads?"

"I hope to never find out." Shouting goodbye to a couple of the other guys in the shop, I made my way to the office to grab Corey so we could get to Dad's. He'd called the day before, saying his most interested buyer was coming by and asking if Corey and I could spare a couple of hours to do some cosmetic work around the place to show that he was dedicated to making whatever improvements were necessary. It felt a little like putting lipstick on a pig, but whatever. Dad rarely asked us for anything, so we jumped at the chance to help when we could.

"Ready to go?" I asked when I entered the office.

Corey was shuffling through some paperwork at his desk. "Almost," he mumbled.

"We're going to be late."

He ignored me, which always drove me crazy. A fact he knew. It made me want to brain him with the stapler sitting on his desk. "Come on. We gotta go."

Instead of getting up, he dropped the papers he held and leaned back in his chair, putting his arms behind his head. "Does that commanding voice work with Zara?"

"Who's Zara?" Jayce asked as he walked in—because of course he'd walk in at that moment—and headed for his own desk.

"Our boy Colton here has himself a fuck buddy. Or, wait... since she thinks you're me, does that make her *my* fuck buddy?"

The thought of Corey having sex with Zara made a twinge of irritation arc beneath my skin. "Screw you."

That made Corey's eyebrows shoot up, and a pleased smile spread across his lips.

Out of my periphery, I saw Jayce's head move back and forth between us. "I'm so confused right now."

"Allow me to enlighten you," Corey eagerly offered.

"Or not," I said, the warning clear in my voice. Not that that had ever stopped Corey before.

But as he studied me for a moment, a weird look passed over his face. "Fine. Have it your way," he said to me.

"What? No way!" Jayce yelled. "You can't leave me hanging like that."

Corey stood and walked over to me, bringing his hand up to squeeze the back of my neck. "Sorry, man. It's twin code." Which wasn't a thing, but for once, my brother didn't seem to want to piss me off.

"Twin code? What the fuck is that?" Jayce asked.

"I'd tell you, but then I'd have to kill you," Corey said as he grabbed his coat and shrugged it on before tossing mine to me.

"Is it like where one of you can feel what's happening to the other? Is that what this is about? Is Colton banging some chick and you can, like, feel it too?" Jayce's eyes were wide, like he'd just discovered Atlantis. "Because that would be badass."

"Jesus Christ," I muttered, rubbing a hand over my face.

"Yes," Corey deadpanned. "That is exactly what we're talking about."

"Why couldn't I have been a twin?" Jayce muttered.

"I can't believe I actually work with you idiots."

Corey barked out a laugh. "Oh, come on. Your life would be so boring without us. Especially without me, since you wouldn't even be getting laid."

I swatted at his head, which he dodged.

"Later, Jayce," he called over his shoulder as he left the office. "Don't forget to make sure you watch Wes leave."

"I may be an idiot, but I'm not a moron."

"Pretty sure it's worse to be an idiot than a moron," I yelled.

"Only you would know the difference," he retorted, causing me to chuckle as Corey and I left the shop and climbed into my truck.

It only took about thirty minutes to get to the restaurant, and Dad had a list waiting for us. We unloaded the tools I'd brought and got to work. After about an hour or so, my dad popped his head into the kitchen, where Corey and I were fixing a latch on one of the freezer doors.

"Hey, guys. The potential buyer is here. I'm going to bring her through."

"'Kay," I grunted as I tried to pry the defective latch off.

"Let me do it, fuckwad. You're going to break the whole door," Corey argued.

"Corey!" Dad scolded.

"Well, he is," he said under his breath.

"Just do me a favor and don't say anything offensive while she's here, all right?"

Corey nodded solemnly. "I'll do my best."

Dad rolled his eyes before disappearing around the corner.

"Can you not drive him crazy? He's going through enough without your shit," I said, finally working the latch free.

"Please. I'm the comedic relief in this family. You'd both be surly assholes without me."

"If you say so."

We'd just finished screwing the new latch into place

when I heard my dad's voice. "My sons are making some improvements to the kitchen as we speak."

"Your...sons are here?" the female voice asked.

It took me a second to recognize the voice as familiar and an additional few seconds to figure out where I knew it from. By the time I spun around, Dad was standing in the kitchen next to his potential buyer. "Fuck my life," I whispered, which caused Corey to straighten beside me.

"Holy shit," he breathed.

"Boys, I think you know Zara Pierce, right? Zara, you remember my sons, C—"

"Yeah," Corey interrupted. "Yup, definitely, for sure, we know Zara. How ya been? Good? That's good."

So smooth, Corey. Though I had to admit, I appreciated him trying to save my ass.

Zara looked between us, and I willed her not to see the truth. Despite my intentions to tell her, I couldn't have her find out here, in front of my dad. What a fucking disaster that would be. Her gaze settled on me, and heat blasted through her eyes. So she really was able to tell us apart. Kind of. In the biblical sense at least.

My dad looked quizzically at Corey but spoke as if his sons weren't making this moment awkward as hell. "I was just showing Zara some of the upgrades we were doing."

"I'm impressed by the progress," she said, smiling at me.

And while part of me wanted to return that smile, another part of me was pissed. She'd never said a word to me about buying my family's restaurant. Granted, we didn't do a whole lot of talking while we were together—and I was a hypocrite for being angry at her for lying—but still. What the fuck?

The smile slid off her face as if she could read my thoughts, but I was saved from having to address it because my dad said started yammering on about the amenities of the kitchen, and Corey grabbed me and hauled me out of there under the guise of us moving on to the next project.

"See you later, Zara," Corey said as he pulled me after him by the arm.

I stayed silent, but I did look over at her before leaving the kitchen. She looked worried, and I didn't like seeing her that way. I nodded at her, and some of the tension seemed to drain from her posture.

I followed Corey out to my truck and watched him lean against it and rub a hand over his face. "Dude, what the fuck?"

My thoughts exactly.

ZARA

Watching CJ leave the kitchen made my chest hurt in a way I hadn't expected. It wasn't that I'd wanted to intentionally keep my interest in his dad's restaurant a secret. But we hadn't crossed the line into sharing personal information. I could admit this might look calculated, since I was the one who always put the kibosh on talking, even though that wasn't my reason.

Mostly it stemmed from the same reason that prevented me from telling my family about it—I didn't want to have anything but positive vibes going into this deal. It was the first time that I was buying a restaurant as the sole investor. I'd piggybacked on a few other deals and learned the tricks of the trade from more seasoned restaurateurs, but this was the first time I'd be going it alone, and I desperately wanted it to be a success.

I wasn't sure how CJ felt about his dad selling, and I didn't want it to get unnecessarily complicated. Which maybe would have led a smarter person to not get involved with him at all. But hey, I was only human.

Besides, there was no promise that I was going to buy this place. I definitely had plans to branch out on my own, but while Maggie's seemed to be a good fit, I hadn't committed to it yet. So why bother discussing something that could easily become a nonissue? And why did it even matter anyway? It wasn't like we were dating. A couple of hot-as-hell encounters did not a relationship make.

"Did you want to come into the office so I can answer any questions you still have, Zara?" CJ's dad, Curtis, said.

Dragging my eyes away from the door CJ had left through, I focused on Curtis. "I don't think that's necessary." I extended my hand toward him, and he shook it. "I appreciate you taking the time to show me your renovation plans. I have some meetings lined up this week with my accountant and real estate agent, but I'll likely be in touch within the next couple of weeks."

"Sounds good," he replied with the kind of smile that clearly came easily to him.

Curtis Jensen was obviously a good man, and it made me want to buy his restaurant all the more. But I couldn't make any snap decisions. My accountant Marty would kill me. So instead, I said my goodbyes and ventured outside, simultaneously hoping I would and would *not* run into CJ.

The decision was taken out of my hands when I saw him leaning against my car. He looked like a romance cover model standing there with his legs crossed at the ankles, arms crossed over his chest, and his head bowed. He must have heard me approach because he lifted his head, and his green eyes caught mine. We stood there staring at each other for a moment before he spoke.

"So you're the buyer, huh?"

Taking a deep breath, I walked over and stood beside him, sinking back onto the car for support. "Maybe. I haven't made any commitments yet."

"Is that why you didn't tell me?"

"I didn't tell you because I didn't want to blur the lines. This is business, and I didn't want you to think I was trying to tie you up in it in some way."

"Gotcha." He straightened abruptly, like I'd said the wrong thing, but I wasn't sure how the truth could be either right or wrong. It was what it was.

"I wasn't trying to mislead you or anything," I tried to explain. "I'm attracted to you, and I wanted to keep that in its own lane, separate from the restaurant stuff. I'm sorry if my doing that upset you."

Rubbing a hand roughly through his hair, he looked like he wanted to bolt. And for the life of me, I wasn't sure why the idea of him doing that bothered me so much. We weren't even friends.

He exhaled a breath before saying, "Look, I know I'm kind of being a bitch about this. This is all...a lot. We just found out my dad was selling this place, and then you walk in, and I know you don't owe me any explanations, but it also seems like something you actively chose not to tell me, and I'm not sure what to do with that."

I wasn't sure how to reply to that in a way that wouldn't make things worse, so I went with what I usually fell back on: brutal honesty. "I did choose not to tell you, because, to be frank—and I'm sorry if this is too blunt—it's not any of your business. At least not on my end of things. I don't even talk about my business decisions with my *family*. I'm sure as hell not going to bring it up as some kind of pillow talk." I kept my voice soft but firm.

I wasn't trying to be dismissive of his feelings, but I wasn't going to accept guilt when I didn't deserve it either. I awaited his response anxiously, unsure how he'd take what I'd said. We'd had a good time together, and I didn't want that to crash and burn over this. But that ball was in his court.

"I get that. I do." His reply made me breathe a little easier, especially since there was no anger or malice in his tone. "This place..." He shook his head.

Moving closer, I put a hand on his arm. "I know the restaurant means a lot to you. I remember eating here occasionally with my parents and watching your mom bustle from table to table, always making sure everyone was enjoying their meal. That's what drew me to Maggie's. The love she had for it. I want to be able to share in that. I want to move around the tables of my restaurant with the same confidence and joy that she did."

CJ stared up at the restaurant, and I stared up at him. After who knows how long, he turned toward me, the movement making my hand slide off his arm. "She really did love this place."

Every word I could have offered seemed inadequate, so I stayed silent.

Placing his hands gently on my shoulders, he leaned in and put a soft kiss on my cheek before pulling back just enough so he could look into my eyes. "If you do decide to buy, take care of it for her."

"I will. I promise."

Squeezing my shoulders, he offered me a small smile before pulling away and stepping around me.

I turned toward him, letting him take a few steps before saying, "This feels like a goodbye."

If I could've pulled the words back into my mouth, I would've. They'd spilled out before my brain had even processed thinking them, and I didn't like how needy they made me sound. Though I also couldn't deny that I wanted to know where we stood after all of this. Not knowing for sure would drive me insane.

Twisting around, he began to walk backward as he winked and said, "You know where to find me."

Once he was out of sight, I slumped back against my car again and took a deep breath. So there was still the possibility of more sexy times with CJ. Despite the warm feeling that spread through my body at the thought, I wasn't totally sure whether that was a good or bad thing. Maybe it would be better to just walk away now before things got any more complicated.

Or maybe it would be better to sleep with him a few more times. Surely he'd work himself out of my system eventually. Wouldn't he?

CHAPTER NINE

COLTON

Corey had been suspiciously quiet on the drive home. Usually he couldn't resist running his mouth or asking questions about every damn thing, but that wasn't the case after we'd had our run-in with Zara, and his silence was freaking me out. Finally, when we trudged through the front door of our apartment and took off our coats, I turned to him. "Okay, let me have it."

"Let you have what?"

"Your unsolicited two cents."

Corey shrugged, a gesture that was too casual to be genuine. It was as if we were on a date and he was playing hard to get—which he surely wasn't.

"Stop being an asshole and tell me how much I fucked up."

His lips quirked as he walked into the kitchen. "And here I thought I was avoiding being an asshole by keeping my mouth shut. I always get that wrong." He opened the refrigerator and withdrew a bottle of water. "What did she say when you talked to her?" he asked after he'd drained half the bottle.

I slid onto the countertop across from where he stood. "That she didn't keep it from me to be shady. Basically, she didn't want to mix business with pleasure."

My brother scoffed. "Too bad that now her pleasure is

wrapped up in our dad's business."

"Nah, she seems capable of keeping the lines from blurring. Not that it matters."

"Why doesn't it matter?"

"Because I gotta end it now." I hadn't said that to Zara when I'd had the chance, but the drive home cemented that it was the right thing to do. Not telling her the truth was already wearing on me, but I couldn't keep it up now that the stakes were even higher. "I should've told her the truth today when I had the chance. Maybe it wouldn't have seemed as bad since she withheld information too."

"Were you dropped on your head as a child?"

"No?" My confusion over what he'd said caused the word to come out as a question, a fact my brother didn't fail to capitalize on.

"I'm glad you sound unsure, because that means it's probably likely, and that explains a lot."

Jumping off the counter, I went to move around him. "I don't know why I even bother talking to you about anything."

Corey grabbed my arm, causing my head to swing toward him. The two of us fucked around a lot, but we rarely put our hands on each other like he was doing. "Dude, you can't tell her the truth, and you can't ghost her either. You'll cost Dad the deal."

I ripped my arm from his grasp and stepped into his space. "First of all, don't grip me up like that again. Second, earlier you didn't want Dad to sell. Seems to me like her pulling out of the deal would suit you just fine."

"Okay, tough guy, de-puff your chest there. I *don't* want Dad to sell, but what I want doesn't matter here. If it's what he wants, what he needs, then I support it. And that includes making sure your clueless girlfriend is happy with everything."

Was I hearing him correctly? "Are you telling me to keep sleeping with some girl, *lying* to her, so she'll go through with a business deal?"

"Yes, that's exactly what I'm telling you."

"You realize that basically makes me a gigolo."

"Don't flatter yourself. It just makes you the same guy you were last time you had sex with her. It wasn't an issue then, so why is it now?"

Unable to stop myself, I shoved him back into the counter. "Fuck you, asshole. You know I've wanted to tell her. I just... I can't..." I yanked my hair as I growled my frustration. "I never meant to lie or to keep lying. I'm not that guy."

"Because you're clearly super fucking emo right now, I'm going to let that shove slide." His face softened. "And I know you're not that guy. Your heart's a damn good size bigger than your brain, that's for sure."

I rolled my eyes, which made him smile.

"For real though, I get that this whole situation has been FUBAR from the beginning, but walking away now could not only fuck things up for Dad but also..."

"But also what?"

He took a deep breath and locked his eyes—same shade of green as mine—on me. "But also for you. I don't think you want to walk away. Be honest with yourself. It wasn't that you didn't have the time or opportunity to tell her. You didn't *want* to tell her. Maybe mostly because you like banging her, but I don't doubt there's more to it than that. Tell me I'm wrong."

"You're wrong. We fucked. That's it. We barely even talk."

"Then why did you look like I set your puppy on fire and dry-humped its corpse when you said you weren't going to see her anymore?"

My brow furrowed. "You have a really messed-up imagination." But his words gave me pause. Had I looked like that? I hadn't meant to. There wasn't more to my feelings for Zara than I'd said. Was there?

No, I resolutely decided. Even if she was someone I *could* like, I didn't know enough about her to actually have those feelings. And besides, relationships weren't my thing. Casual hookups, no problem. But the thought of more made me break out in a sweat. "I like her as a human being. She's a good person. But I don't want to date her or anything."

Corey eyed me dubiously, but he didn't comment on it. Instead, he said, "Listen, Dad never asks us for anything. I'm not telling you to keep sleeping with her, but I am telling you not to do anything that will cost Dad the sale."

"That's basically telling me to sleep with her."

"I've told you no such thing. But she clearly likes the D. As long as you give her some solid orgasms, she makes out on the deal."

"You're very cavalier about whoring me out."

He brought his hand up to grip my neck and gave it a squeeze—a gentler one this time. "I'm cavalier about a lot of things, but not about our family. You and Dad are all I have. So if you can't see Zara anymore, then we'll find another way to help Dad out."

Silence stretched between us for a minute, both of us running through our absolute truths and letting those things pass between us. We always put our family first. We always had each other's back. And we always were honest with each other. The moment spread until we both took deep breaths and soaked up the fact that we were back on solid ground.

"You're trying to use reverse psychology on me, aren't you?"

"Is it working?"

"Yeah, it's working."

He gave my neck a pat before pulling back. "What do you want for dinner?"

It was his version of a peace offering, and I'd take it. Especially since I had my own atoning to do. I was pretty sure I was lying to him and myself, even if I hadn't said the lie out loud.

Was my unwillingness to keep deceiving Zara because it was fundamentally wrong? Or was it because I wanted her to want the real me?

CHAPTER TEN

COLTON

I'd spent most of the next two weeks at the bike shop and hadn't seen Zara since the restaurant. Tonight that was supposed to change. She'd texted a few times to meet up, and though my dick wanted to say hell yes, my brain—in some strange stroke of adulthood—interfered. And my conscience, that bastard, was even worse. Because no matter how hard I tried to convince myself that Corey's logic was sound and the right decision for our family, keeping up the charade was wearing on me.

Especially when Zara had texted to ask me to come to her house after I finished up at the shop. But Corey was right. I couldn't tell Zara the truth yet, and I couldn't break things off with her either.

And as much as I hated to admit it, I didn't want to.

We were behind on both bikes we were building, and I hated the possibility that I might not meet a deadline I'd been the one to make. It was a promise just like any other that I felt I needed to fulfill. It didn't matter if I had to work until one in the morning, as I had the past two nights. I had no plans of letting one of our customers down.

When Saturday rolled around and we still weren't done, I offered Wes overtime if he wanted to work for a few hours with me. The guy was never one to pass up an opportunity for overtime, but more than that, he wasn't one to leave a friend when that friend needed him.

"You need me tomorrow too?" Wes asked. "I can come by for a few hours, finish things up if you want."

I glanced at the clock on the wall. Just past seven. I tossed the wrench on a nearby table and pulled my phone out.

> *Have to work late tonight, but I'll make it up to you tomorrow morning. Pancakes?*

Is pancakes code for sex?
Because covering you in syrup
sounds delicious in sooo many ways.

> *Uh...I was legitimately talking about breakfast, but I'd be lying if I said your version didn't sound good too.*

So you're planning to cook for me?
I could get on board with that. ;)

> *I was actually thinking diner food might be a better option than my cooking. I'm not sure my culinary expertise is up to your professional standards.*

I was also worried that being in the house with Zara might lead to more sex. And while that wasn't a negative—not really—it didn't do anything to help the guilt I felt either.

Sunday mornings are for being lazy

around the house. No matter how
horrible your cooking skills are.

In that case, pancakes it is.

Well, SEX and pancakes.
Gotta work off those carbs ;)

That had me laughing.

LOL. Sex and Pancakes...
Sounds like the title of a song.

"Who are you texting?" Wes asked, and I realized he'd probably been staring at me for the better part of my conversation with Zara. "You look like someone just promposed to you."

"I don't even think that can be used as a verb" was all I could come up with, but Wes's comment got me thinking. Despite the fact that I felt horrible about lying to Zara, interacting with her in any way made me stupidly happy— emphasis on the "stupid" part.

He leaned back in the stool he was sitting on and looked up at me from across the bike. "Avoiding the question, I see." He raised an eyebrow at me as he waited for an answer. But this fucker wasn't getting one. He might be a friend, but I wasn't about to talk to him about my...whatever it was with Zara.

"Stop staring at me like that creepy fuck from that stalker show, and get back to work."

"Or what?" Wes said, more amused than he should be by his boss.

"Or you're fired," I threatened, though I knew he knew

better than to believe me.

He smiled and then lowered his gaze back to the task at hand. "We both know you're too damn happy to fire me," he said.

And as I walked toward the office to finish my conversation with Zara in private, I hated how right he was.

ZARA

I hadn't seen CJ in two weeks, and it was nearly killing me. We hadn't talked much since the restaurant incident, and my anxiety about it had reached a new level the past few days. I didn't know if he was avoiding me intentionally or just really busy with work. Or maybe both.

He'd seemed friendly, even flirty, when we'd texted earlier, and I hoped that meant his shock—or anger—about my purchasing the restaurant had dissipated enough that we could find our way back to how we'd been.

Which was hot-as-hell encounters that had me practically begging for more. It occurred to me that I'd pretty much done that exact thing through text earlier when I'd interpreted pancakes as sex, but I was too horny to care. CJ would be here soon, and my body thrummed with anticipation. Two weeks does not a dry spell make, but my vagina had been arguing that fact recently.

When the doorbell rang, I practically sprinted out of the kitchen to the front door, flinging it open to reveal the sexiness I'd missed over the past few weeks. In worn jeans stained with grease and a tight black T-shirt with their company's logo on it.

"Hi," I said. My voice sounded more timid than I would've liked for it to, as if my next move was contingent on his response.

"Hey," he replied, and he wiped a hand across his forehead, smudging a speck of black that was there. I stepped away from the door so he could enter, and he kicked off his work boots before going any farther into the house. "Sorry. I came straight from work. I was worried if I stopped home for a shower, you might already be asleep when I got here."

I didn't bother telling him there was no way I could have fallen asleep. I was too ramped up, like I'd been shot full of adrenaline and other hormones that resulted in me feeling like a sex-crazed teenager after a night of Red Bulls and cocaine.

"It's okay," I told him. "I have a shower."

His smile formed the beginnings of a laugh before he said, "I may have to take you up on that." Moving closer to me, he extended a hand and reached around my hip to pull me against him. "As long as you don't leave me in there alone," he added against my neck as he ran kisses down toward my chest.

"God, I missed you—missed *this*," I corrected myself.

His "Me too" came out as a moan, and I wondered if he'd picked up on my slip but simply chose to ignore it.

But my brain couldn't concentrate too long on that because my body was currently using every ounce of my energy. I pressed into him, feeling his cock harden against me, and ran my fingers down the cords of muscle on his back and shoulders. This was what a man felt like, and I needed to feel more of him. "Shower," I breathed out as he tugged at my nipple.

"Yes, ma'am," he answered, helping me pull my shirt over my head.

The rest of our clothes came off quickly, like a discarded trail of breadcrumbs that led to the bathroom. But we never actually made it into the shower. It was as if our nudity brought out some sort of animalistic impulse in us that we couldn't ignore. This was how I always felt around CJ—primal and unrestrained. And as he hoisted me up against the wall and drove into me, I may have let out one of the loudest screams in my sexual memory.

He thrust deep and hard, and every push inside me brought both of us closer to an explosion that had been building for two weeks. Even the thought of CJ had my entire body feeling like a bomb, ready to go off at the most innocent touch. And this definitely wasn't innocent. It was uninhibited and passionate and dirty. It was sweaty and loud, and when I couldn't hold back anymore, I came with a scream, grabbing for anything nearby, which happened to be the shower curtain.

I didn't care that I'd pulled it down—tugged it so hard that the tension pole came with it, nearly hitting CJ in the head as he chased his own orgasm. Both of us laughed for a few seconds before composing ourselves enough to finish what we'd started. He was frantic now, pumping into me quickly with shallow drives that let me know he was close. "Come for me," I said, feeling another orgasm building inside me.

"Almost there," he warned, and it was then I realized he hadn't put on a condom. "Fuucck."

"Not yet," I begged, hoping he could hold off a few more seconds now so I could come again.

"What? Seriously? I can't..."

"I'm right there. A little longer."

His face strained, the veins in his neck thickening, his eyes clenched shut as his rhythm stuttered. "Shit," he said. "Please."

And I was coming again—warm waves washing through my body as CJ gave me everything he had. The second I finished, he pulled out, put me down, and then grabbed his cock in his hand to jerk himself. He tugged a few times before come jetted from him and onto my stomach, down my hips. His hand found the wall next to my head when he was done, and within a few seconds, both of us were heaps on the bathroom floor, our backs against the wall.

My head fell onto CJ's shoulder. "I think it's time for that shower now."

Hours later, I was waking up with CJ's warm, hard body—emphasis on hard—wrapped around me. "When did you get here?" I asked. "I didn't even hear you come in."

He tensed at my comment and pulled back from me a little. "Um, Zara," he said, sounding concerned. "What do you mean you didn't hear me come in? You opened the door for me. And then we had sex."

"We did?"

Now he was hovering above my body, his weight propped on his forearms beside me. It made him seem even larger than he was.

"It must not have been that good, or I'd remember it."

"That's not even funny," he said. He plopped down next to me and stared up at the ceiling, the blanket hitting just below his hip bones.

"It is a little bit." I traced the lines of his abs with my nails, feeling the short, soft hairs under my fingertips. Then my mouth found his neck, and I felt the vibration of his laugh and some of the tension he'd been holding release as I kissed him. I could see his erection through the blanket, and I put my hand lightly over it.

"You're ridiculous," he said, grasping my hips and squeezing just enough to make me squeal. He held me there, pinned below him as he tickled me until I had tears running down my cheeks.

He relented to let me catch my breath and then hopped off. Then his eyes grew wide, and he smiled broadly. "Pancake time."

Twenty minutes and one cup of coffee later, we were sitting at my kitchen bar eating the blueberry pancakes CJ had made. "You're a liar," I said, stabbing another pancake with my fork before dropping it onto my plate and drenching it with butter and syrup.

CJ's mouth was full, so he didn't talk. Instead he just looked at me, his mouth ceasing to chew for a moment before he seemed to remember what it was supposed to be doing. A few seconds later, he swallowed hard, forcing his gigantic bite of food down in a way that made me wonder if I'd have to perform the Heimlich maneuver or risk losing him right here in my house.

"You okay?" I asked when he began gulping down hot coffee.

He put the mug down, his face flushed. "Fine, why?" And then before I could answer, "Um, so why am I a liar?"

He took a bite of bacon and then dropped the remainder of the slice on the plate. He didn't look at me, and it made me wonder if I'd done something wrong, though I couldn't imagine what.

"Because you acted like you couldn't cook pancakes, and these are pretty awesome."

He glanced up at me and finished the bite he was chewing before wiping his mouth. "That doesn't make me a liar."

"What would you call it?" I teased.

He thought hard for a second before saying, "It's more like...not telling the truth."

I laughed. "I'm pretty sure that's the dictionary definition of lying."

"Okay, maybe that wasn't the best explanation," he said. "But there is definitely a difference here."

I raised my eyebrows, prompting him to continue. "Am I getting a philosophical CJ?" I had trouble imagining that. "Go on."

"Leading you to believe that I might not be a good cook and *saying* I'm not a good cook are completely different."

"No way." I pulled out my phone. "Let's have a look at the evidence. When I suggested you cook pancakes for me, you wrote, *I'm not sure my culinary expertise is up to your professional standards.* You implied you aren't a good cook."

"I didn't imply *any*thing. You inferred it."

"Semantics," I argued. "That matters zero." I made a circle with my hand and put it up to his face, but it didn't make him laugh like I thought it would.

"It matters completely. Just because I didn't correct your misunderstanding doesn't mean I'm a liar. Maybe I didn't want you to feel bad about your mistake. You know, then it would be all awkward when I saw you again. You'd be embarrassed that you assumed the wrong thing, and I'd feel guilty."

"About *pancakes*?"

"Yes. About pancakes," he repeated, like saying the words out loud made his argument more valid.

I stood from the counter where we'd been eating and grabbed my plate to put in the sink. When I walked back over to him, I gave him a kiss on his forehead. "We're not fighting about pancakes, are we?" I joked.

"No, we're not fighting about anything."

"Good." I smiled. "I'm going to take a shower. Then I'll

clean up, and we can figure out what to do today."

"Sounds good," he said.

"And, CJ?"

"Yeah?"

"Relax. It's just pancakes."

"Right," he said, and as I headed up the stairs, I heard him mutter to himself, "Just pancakes."

COLTON

While Zara was in the shower, I cleaned up the kitchen, searching her cabinets for where the pans, plates, and spatula went. I figured she'd be pleasantly surprised when she came back down. I also needed to distract myself from the whole lying-by-omission thing.

There was obviously no way Zara knew I was really Colton—the brother she thought she couldn't stand but clearly wanted more of. Because if she did, my ass wouldn't still be standing in her kitchen.

She didn't even want me telling little fibs about cooking. She'd probably chop my balls off and serve them as some sort of foreign delicacy if she knew I wasn't Corey. Even the thought made me wince and had me protecting the precious area with my hand as I put away the last of the dishes.

I was drying the counter when the doorbell rang, and I headed over to answer it. "Can I help you?" I asked the woman standing on the other side. She looked professional in a pantsuit and heels, and she was holding two cups of iced coffee.

"Sorry," she said, looking confused. She leaned back to study the numbers to the right of the door. "I thought I might be at the wrong house for a second. Is Zara here?"

"She is. She's in the shower right now. Can I help you with something until she comes down?"

She shifted the coffees to one hand and removed her sunglasses with the other. My instinct was to reach out and grab the drinks because I was pretty sure she was going to drop at least one of them, but I didn't want to make any quick movements that might startle her. She seemed a little on edge as it was.

"You can start by telling me what you're doing at my daughter's house on a Sunday morning wearing sweat pants and... Isn't that called a wifebeater?" She was looking at me like she should be asking me to change her tire.

I was suddenly very aware that my messy hair and lack of real clothing revealed that I'd probably spent the night with this woman's daughter. It made me feel vulnerable in a way I wasn't used to—like I'd been caught stealing candy from a corner store and was trying to pretend I'd just forgotten to pay for it. "I'll grab another shirt" was all I could come up with. "Please, come in."

As we walked through the living room, I grabbed my shirt from last night off the couch and pulled it over my head, remembering how Zara had ripped it off me just as quickly last night—a fact that made the current situation that much more awkward. Reaching a hand out to Zara's mother, I tried to sound composed as I introduced myself. Or introduced CJ, at least. I was surprised I didn't say Colton.

"I'm not sure we've ever met before now, but I've known Zara for a while. My parents owned the restaurant Maggie's over on Madison." If people didn't know who I was, they were usually at least familiar with my parents' restaurant.

"I haven't been there in a long time."

I'd been hoping the familiarity would make Zara's mom feel a little better about the strange man in her daughter's house, but from the look on her face, it didn't. Speaking of her daughter, where the hell was she? This was getting more awkward by the second. Clearly, Mrs. Pierce had no idea that Zara might be buying Maggie's, so I couldn't even pretend that my presence here had something to do with that.

I nodded slowly and then pointed toward the kitchen. "I was just cleaning up from breakfast. Can I make you something? We don't have any pancakes left, but I can make more or cook some eggs or something." *You dumb fuck. Now she knows for sure you slept with her daughter.*

Her expression seemed to soften a bit with the offer. "A man who cooks *and* cleans. Where did Zara find you?"

I smiled. "High school, actually."

"Really? I'm surprised I don't remember you." She laughed, though I could tell she'd been trying not to.

"It's okay. I have one of those super-forgettable faces," I said, making her laugh again.

"You know what? I'll take a cup of coffee while I wait. I brought these for Zara and me, but you can have mine. I didn't drink any of it yet."

"That's nice of you, Mrs. Pierce—"

"Jane. Please."

"Jane. That's nice of you, but I'm really fine." I held up my mug.

"Suit yourself," she said. "But it's a caramel mocha latte. The black stuff you're drinking doesn't really compare."

I looked inside the mug. "You're right. It's missing about six hundred calories and forty grams of sugar."

"Told you," she said with a smile before bringing the straw

to her lips.

We drank our coffee and talked for a few more minutes, mainly about the house she was showing to a couple about a mile or so from here. It made me wonder why Zara hadn't chosen her mother to be her real estate agent for the restaurant transaction, but I wasn't going to ask Jane. She didn't seem to know anything about it, and I was *not* going to be the one to tell her. And I didn't plan to ask Zara either because it was none of my damn business. Clearly there was a reason Zara had chosen to keep her mom out of the loop.

A few minutes later, Zara came downstairs, wearing leggings and a fitted white T-shirt. She hadn't bothered to put on a bra, and as she walked toward the kitchen, I had to force my eyes to meet hers so Jane wouldn't think I was perving on her daughter right in front of her.

"You want to just hang out here today?" she asked as she approached me. "We can spend the day in bed, and—"

"Your mom's here."

As she entered the kitchen, Zara's head whipped to the island, where Jane sat sipping on her coffee. Zara's gaze darted between us. "What are you doing here?"

"Well, that wasn't the greeting I was hoping for."

Zara shook her head and looked at Jane apologetically. "Sorry. I didn't mean it like that. Is everything okay? You never come by without calling first."

"I thought I'd surprise you. I brought you your favorite iced coffee," she said, waving the cup back and forth.

Zara smiled and her shoulders seemed to relax a bit. "Caramel mocha?"

"Half almond milk, half cream," Jane said.

"Thanks." Zara took the coffee from her mom and sat next

to her at the counter. "But seriously, why are you here? You're freaking me out a little."

Her mom laughed. "I didn't mean to. I have a couple who's looking at a house nearby, and I did a drive-by earlier. I have a little time to kill before I have to meet my clients."

"You have to stop calling them drive-bys. It sounds like you're shooting up the neighborhood from the window of your Prius."

"That's ridiculous, Zara."

"I know. That's why you have to stop saying it."

I remained quiet as they talked, but when Jane's gaze went to me, I knew I was about to get involved in the conversation.

"So are you going to introduce me to your boyfriend?"

Zara's mouth opened, presumably to correct her mom, but then she said, "I figured you'd already met."

"Well, we did. But a formal introduction would be nice. I had no idea you were seeing anyone."

Zara and I had a conversation with our eyes—one where we acknowledged that the only way we were "seeing" each other was naked but there was no point in explaining the nuances of our situation to her mother. And my guess was that Zara didn't want to let her mom think she was just sleeping with men she didn't have any intention of having a relationship with. I couldn't say I blamed her.

"Mom, this is Corey. Corey, this is my mother, Jane Pierce."

"Pleasure to meet you again. And you can call me CJ, actually."

Zara looked at me strangely, like she found my choice of a nickname odd in this situation. As far as she knew, it was only people in our high school who referred to my brother and me as CJ.

"Figured I shouldn't confuse people. You call me CJ, so your mom can too."

"Pleasure's mine," Jane said with a smile. Then she took notice of something on the counter and picked up an envelope. "Zara, you haven't RSVP'd for this yet?"

"I kept forgetting to send it. I'm going, though. I called Grandma and told her. You know I wouldn't miss that."

"What is it?" I asked, though I knew it was also something that was none of my business.

"My parents' fiftieth anniversary party," Jane said.

"Fifty. Wow, that's"—*really long*—"impressive," I said, thankfully finding a word that didn't make me sound like an asshole. "What's their secret?"

"You can ask them yourself. I'm sure they'd love to meet you."

"Mom, I haven't asked CJ if he'd go yet."

"Well, ask him now," she said. "He's right here. Grandma and Grandpa aren't getting any younger. I'm sure there's room for one more. They'd love to see you with a boyfriend, don't you think?"

"I'm sure they would, Mom, but CJ's been swamped at work." Zara looked to me. "You have a lot happening at the shop now, right? And it's such short notice. I don't want you to feel obligated."

I honestly had no idea what she wanted me to say. *Why are women so damn complicated?* If I agreed that I was too busy, I looked like one of those pricks who chose work over their girlfriend or wife—not that she was either of those—and if I agreed to go...well, then I'd have to accompany Zara to a family function and pretend to be her boyfriend, Corey.

Fuck my life.

"I'd love to go."

CHAPTER ELEVEN

COLTON

Even a week after my impulsive decision to become Zara's fake boyfriend, I'd still failed to come to terms with the clusterfuck my life had become. Zara and I had continued to bang each other's brains out, because no matter how hard I tried to resist her, my dick was always harder. My intention to slowly pull away from her was easily forgotten with a meet-the-family event on the horizon. I'd promised I'd see this through for her, and I wouldn't fail her. I knew it wouldn't atone for being less than truthful, but it was all I had to offer.

I looked around my room to see if I'd missed anything before zipping up my duffel and turning toward my doorway, where Corey was leaning. "What?" I asked as I pushed past him and walked toward the foyer.

"I'm just curious how you do it," Corey said, his voice full of mock wonder.

"Do what?" I didn't really want to know.

"Get yourself into such fucked-up situations."

I dropped my bag by the door and started toward the kitchen to grab a couple bottles of water. "Well, since I'm pretending to be you, I'd really expect no less."

"No way, man. This is some epic fucking up. I've never come close to meeting my fuck buddy's entire family while pretending to be someone else."

Rolling my eyes, I opened the fridge and withdrew a few bottles. "I'm not pretending to be someone else. I'm being me but with a different name."

Corey wagged his finger at me. "I'm liking how delusional you're becoming. Believing your own bullshit is a new high. Or low. Whatever."

I grabbed a small cooler and slammed it onto the counter before whirling around on him. "Why are you giving me shit about this? You're the one who told me to keep lying. And you know how much I hate doing it, so why do you keep harping on me about it? I feel like enough of an asshole without you piling on." After tossing the waters into the cooler, I stormed back toward the foyer. I'd wait outside for Zara to pick me up. Fuck my fucking brother.

"Yo, Colt. Wait, man."

Ignoring him, I shouldered my bag and opened our front door, but he stepped in front of me and pushed his body back against the door so it closed again.

"Move," I practically growled.

"I'm sorry. I was trying to loosen you up. Be the comedic relief. I wasn't trying to piss you off."

"Yeah, well, you're shit at reading a situation."

"Noted." He didn't move.

"Do you need a hug and kiss goodbye or something? Move so I can go."

"She's not even here yet."

"I know, but I don't want her to come up. Seeing us together might tip her off."

"It didn't at the restaurant or at the gym."

"I don't want to tempt fate." I reached for the knob, but he batted my hand away.

"Don't leave mad, snookums."

"Jesus Christ, what even is my life right now?" I muttered. "I'm not mad. Now get out of the way."

"Your words say you're not mad, but your eyes say you're plotting my untimely death."

"I don't know if 'untimely' is the word I'd use. I actually think it's long past due."

"Be honest." Corey's face was serious, as was his tone. "If I died, would you become me full-time?"

I shoved him as he began cackling. "You're such a dick." But my words had no heat behind them because I was trying my best not to laugh along with him. My phone chimed, and I dug into my pocket to pull it out. "She's here. I gotta go."

He moved so I could open the door, but he began speaking again before I could get away from him. "Just...if you need me, make sure you call, okay? No matter what time."

"You make it sound like I'm spending the weekend with the Voorhees family. I'll be fine. I'm a big boy."

"Probably even bigger now that you've assumed my identity," he said as he waggled his eyebrows.

"You wish."

Once I was outside, I spotted Zara's red SUV and made my way over to it. After throwing my bag in the trunk, I slid into the passenger seat. "Hey."

"Hey. Ready for the worst family reunion of your life?"

"You really know how to sell it." I chuckled. "You sure you don't mind driving?" Truth be told, I'd much rather be behind the wheel, but she'd insisted. Though it couldn't hurt to ask one more time.

"Nah, I know the way. It'll be easier if I drive."

I wanted to argue that it actually probably wouldn't be easier because I made a shitty passenger, but I kept my mouth shut. "How long of a drive is it?" I asked.

"Just under three hours, so we should be there by noon. Usually when I leave at this time, I manage to miss any heavy traffic, though you never know what Fridays may bring."

I sank back into my seat. "Sounds good."

"You can put whatever you want on the radio," she offered.

"You like Howard Stern?" I asked as I switched to his station on Sirius. "Sometimes music on a long drive makes me fall asleep."

"Like a toddler?" she asked, a small smile playing on her lips that I wanted to kiss away.

"Yup."

"Stern's fine with me," she said.

We let the talk-radio show fill the silence, making random comments here and there about their discussion.

But about an hour in, Zara switched off the radio. "We should probably talk about how we're going to tackle this weekend."

I took a deep breath. All of this premeditated lying was wearing on me. "Okay, shoot."

"How comfortable are you with PDA? Because I don't want to make you uncomfortable, but I don't want it to seem weird that we don't touch or anything."

"Considering the places our mouths have been, I'm pretty sure some casual touching and kissing won't make me head for the hills."

"I figured but didn't want to assume."

"I appreciate that. But PDA away. I'm game for whatever."

"So I can molest you on the dance floor at the party?" she asked.

"Can you molest the willing?"

She laughed, which was what I'd been hoping for. She seemed tense, and since it was my fault—again—that we were in this situation, I wanted to make it up to her. I'd be whatever she needed me to be this weekend. It was the least I could do.

ZARA

The last half of the drive was spent reviewing our backstory. We'd decided to keep it simple and go with what had actually happened, but with more emphasis on a relationship than two people casually screwing. We had some random "get to know you" conversations, and before I knew it, we were pulling up the winding drive that led to my grandparents' farm.

"Whoa, this is incredible," CJ said.

I glanced over at him and smiled at his widened eyes and swiveling head. The land truly was beautiful. The three-hundred-plus acres were mostly taken up by the apple orchard, but my grandparents also grew other fruit and had some animals on the premises. They also operated a market and had seasonal activities, but they closed all of that at the end of November.

Putting the car in park, I sank back against my seat and gazed out the window. "I loved coming up here as a kid. I mean, don't get me wrong, the family on my mom's side is...quirky and quick to voice their opinions. But they're kind too. Solid, dependable people who work hard and love harder."

"Sounds great," CJ said.

I turned and found him looking at me sweetly. I smiled back. "It's completely smothering. But they mean well."

A commotion had me turning toward the house, where

I saw a small crowd of family gathering on the front stoop, shivering as they stared us down. "Ready to face the firing squad?"

CJ pushed open his door. "Your optimism is one of my favorite things about you."

Laughing, I got out of the car.

"About time you all got here. These nosy turkeys have had their faces pressed to my windows all morning," my grandma yelled.

"Oh please, Mom. You're the one who just yelled to all of us that they were here."

"That's my aunt Lindy. She and my grandma have been arguing since Lindy emerged from the womb."

"Lindy the Arguer. Got it," he said as he grabbed our bags.

"Here, I can grab mine." I reached for my suitcase, but he pulled it away from me.

"What kind of boyfriend would I be if I didn't carry your bags?" He looked as if the very notion was scandalizing, and I grinned at him. He really was stupidly handsome. My family was going to eat him alive.

"Joel," Grandma bellowed. "Go help them with their things."

Even though he was older than me, Lindy's oldest son didn't hesitate to obey Grandma's command like he was a kid. "Hey, Joelly," I said as he walked into my arms for a hug.

"Hey, Zare-bear." He extricated himself from me and extended a hand toward CJ. "And you must be the infamous CJ, here to keep Zara from becoming a spinster."

I smacked my cousin's arm, which only made both men laugh.

"Let me take those from you. I'll never hear the end of it

if I let a guest carry his own bags," Joel said, only half kidding.

Once he'd started toward the house, CJ caught my eye. *Zare-bear*, he mouthed.

"Call me that and I will bury you in the orchard."

He laughed at me again, the bastard. The bitter cold had sent most of my family back into the house, but my grandma remained. When we reached her, I hugged her tightly. She was crazy as a loon, but damn did I love her. She always smelled faintly of apples and cinnamon and hugged like she hadn't seen you in decades.

"How've you been, darling?" she asked quietly.

"Good," I said, pulling back. "Really good."

She smiled broadly at me before turning to CJ. I opened my mouth to introduce him properly, but she beat me to it. "And you're CJ, I presume. I'm Zara's grandmother. Name's Mable, but you can call me Meemaw."

Tilting my head a bit to see if that would help me process her words, I watched as she leaned in to hug CJ. When they separated, I asked, "Why would he call you Meemaw? No one has ever called you that."

"I know, but I always liked it. Figured this would be my only chance to try it on for size. Come on in. I got hot apple cider in the kitchen."

We stared after her before looking at each other. I shrugged. "Well, that wasn't as weird as I'd anticipated."

CJ's face slackened a bit in surprise, but I didn't dwell on it. Following my grandma to the kitchen, I braced myself for what awaited us. Most of my mom's family lived and worked on the farm, so I had no doubt they'd all be here. And I wasn't disappointed.

It was almost comical how casual they were all trying

to appear. My uncle Hank was inspecting a spot on the floor with his boot while my aunt Lindy wiped the spotless counter. Their daughter Abigail was leafing through a magazine while their other son Bobby—who was a few years younger than Joel—shook the table, seemingly trying to see if it wobbled. My own mom and dad stood together with my sister and her husband looking at a painting of the orchard that had been hanging in that exact spot for as long as I could remember. And my grandpa and Uncle Travis were opening and closing a kitchen cupboard that seemed to be doing its job just fine.

The scene looked like a typical family congregated at the hub of the house. Except you could've heard a damn pin drop. It was like walking onto the set of *Get Out* if the movie's goal had been to lure city boys into the farm life.

I cleared my throat. "Hi, everyone. This is CJ. CJ, this is... everyone."

And with those words, my family came to life. It was as if CJ's appearance was some kind of surprise gift none of them had known they wanted until they'd received it. It was a horde of shaking hands and exchanged pleasantries. Even I was overwhelmed by their convergence, and I knew these people.

CJ held his own, though. Plastering a wide smile on his face, he shook every hand and answered every question thrown at him. From what he did for a living to where he lived, no scrap of personal information was safe from my very own information army.

Joel reemerged and said, "I put your stuff in the Chuckie room."

Groaning, I very nearly whined, "Why did we get the Chuckie room?"

"Last to arrive..." Joel ended the statement with a smirk,

which I wanted to smack off him.

My grandmother waggled a finger at us. "I told all of you to stop calling it that."

"What's the Chuckie room?" CJ asked. When Grandma scowled at him, he added, "Sorry...Meemaw." His lips stumbled over the name, as if he wasn't sure he should actually use it or not.

"Who's Meemaw?" Uncle Travis whispered, though his voice was so deep, the words rumbled through the entire kitchen anyway.

Ignoring him, I turned to CJ. "The china doll room is where Grandma's collection of porcelain dolls is stored. In their various states."

"Various states?" CJ asked, looking confused and a little wary. He would deserve a nationally recognized award after the weekend.

Joel cut in. "Think of it as more of a doll hospital. Grandma...or Meemaw?" He turned his attention momentarily to my grandmother. "Is that a thing we're calling you now? I'm into it." Shifting his gaze back to CJ, he continued. "Meemaw over there buys dolls and uses them for parts on her more prestigious ones."

"I wouldn't say prestigious. Some just mean a little more to me is all," Grandma clarified.

"When they come to life, it's going to be like a zombie army," Bobby muttered. "We're all goners."

CJ looked a little pale. "So we have to...sleep...in the room with the...dolls?"

"I wouldn't," Bobby warned.

"All of you stop right now," Grandma scolded. "Those dolls are beautiful and wouldn't hurt a hair on your heads."

All of us paused and looked around at one another, but by seemingly unanimous agreement, no one commented on the fact that she'd just implied the dolls did in fact come to life.

"It'll be fine," I said, attempting to reassure CJ. "I've slept in there a few times. It's no big deal."

CJ didn't look convinced, but he offered me a small smile anyway. I hoped he'd still be able to smile once this weekend was over.

CHAPTER TWELVE

COLTON

Zara didn't let the interrogation in the kitchen go for much longer. She pulled me away so we could freshen up. I wasn't sure I'd ever freshened up before, but I was only too happy to start.

"Sorry about them," she whispered when we'd started up the stairs toward the bedroom. "They're just excited. I haven't brought anyone up here before."

The words warmed me even though they shouldn't have. She hadn't brought me here willingly. But still, the fact that I was the first made me feel proud to be there. "No worries. I like them." And I did. They were intense and maybe a little crazy, but there was obviously a lot of love between them. My family was incredibly small: just Corey, Dad, me, and an aunt who lived in Florida who we never saw. It was fun seeing how the other half lived.

"They like you too. Which I should've considered, since they'll probably be bummed when I tell them we broke up."

There was a pang in my chest at her words. It felt like maybe I would be bummed too, which made no kind of sense since we weren't even together. "Let's worry about that when we have to," I said, hoping to convince myself as much as her.

I followed her down a hallway that had green walls

adorned with family pictures. She stopped at a door and put her back to it, looking distinctly uncomfortable. "I'm not sure how to prepare you for this room," she blurted out.

"You could try just letting me see it."

Biting her lip, she seemed to ponder that as she looked at the floor. "It's a little...jarring."

"Zara." I waited until she lifted her eyes to meet mine. "Open the door."

Without turning around, she twisted the knob and pushed the door open. Since she didn't move from the doorway, I had to practically push through her to get into the room. But once I was inside, I understood why she'd been nervous.

"Holy shit," I whispered.

"We can stay at a hotel," she said.

"This is... Wow." There were dolls on every surface. And there were *a lot* of surfaces. Dressers, desks, and tables were all around the room, with dolls standing, sitting in rocking chairs, having tea, and every fucking thing in between. But that wasn't the worst of it. There were also doll *parts* hanging from clothesline strung across the room in a seemingly haphazard fashion. "It's like a *Pet Sematary* for dolls."

Zara nodded as she looked at the porcelain mortuary above our heads. "It's definitely a thing of nightmares."

"I hope you weren't hoping to have sex in this room. Because I'm pretty sure this is going to haunt my dick for a long time."

A laugh burst out of her, which was what I'd been hoping for. She'd been looking worried as we stood there, and there was really no need to be. Yeah, this was weird as hell, but it was also going to make for a great story when I got home. As long as these dolls didn't actually come to life and slaughter me in my sleep.

Moving in front of me, Zara slid her arms around my neck and pressed her body into mine. "Think I can help it get over its fears?"

Judging by the twitch I felt in my jeans, I was pretty sure she could. But where was the fun in admitting that? "I don't know. I think it would take considerable protection from the demonic forces in this room for him to consider getting with the program."

She looked up at me through long, thick lashes, and my cock was suddenly completely with the program. A fact she must've felt but ignored for the sake of the scene we were letting play out. "What if I kissed it? Would it feel better then?"

Jesus fucking Christ. The image of Zara on her knees with her mouth on my cock made my groin throb with want. I had to clear my throat before I could push words past my lips. "I think that would be a solid way to start." My voice was raspy. There was no denying it—this woman really did it for me.

She dropped her hands to my waistband and slipped the button free before dragging the zipper down. Keeping her gaze on mine, she pushed my jeans and boxers down to midthigh before slowly lowering to her knees. The look she gave me was seductive before she turned her attention to my cock. She put a soft kiss on the flushed head, which caused a moan to rumble up from my chest and fly out of my mouth. I ripped my sweater over my head so I could see her better because I had a feeling I wasn't going to want to miss a second.

Wrapping a hand around the base of my erection, she began licking my dick like it was a lollipop. Intermittently she would swirl her tongue around the head, which felt amazing, but it wasn't enough. My cock needed to be enveloped by the heat of her mouth.

Her eyes sparkled like she knew exactly what I wanted, but she wasn't going to give it to me anytime soon.

"Please," I groaned.

"Please what?" she asked, looking at me innocently. She was more evil than the creepy-ass dolls surrounding us.

"Do...more," I answered stupidly because evidently all my focus was farther south than my brain.

"Hmm." The hum vibrated up my shaft, and my head fell back before I remembered I wanted to watch. She took her mouth off me long enough to say, "I'm not sure what 'more' is. You're going to need to be more specific." Her voice was soft and calm. She worked her tongue on my balls for a second before resuming her torture on my dick.

I tangled my hand in her hair, pulling it just enough to let her know I was approaching the end of my rope with her teasing. Even though I wasn't—not really. Sex with Zara was fun in a way it hadn't ever been for me before. It wasn't just a means to an end. With her, the means mattered almost as much. Getting off was the cherry on an already delicious sundae.

But the way her eyelids fluttered closed when I tugged on her hair let me know that she was into the role reversal, which made me into it as well. "Zara." I ordered her to look at me for the second time in about five minutes, and watching her gaze instantly cut to mine made my arousal hit new heights. Tightening my grip on her hair a bit, I said, "Suck me."

Her lips fell open on a moan, and she plunged down on me, taking as much of my shaft into her mouth as she could. She bobbed on me with urgency, as if she was enjoying it as much as I was, which didn't seem possible. Sliding into her wet mouth was heaven, and even though I'd never imagined an afterlife with doll corpses surrounding me, I wasn't in the least put off by it. I'd happily stay in this room forever if it meant getting more blowjobs like this.

"Fucking beautiful," I whispered as I watched her devour me.

She whimpered, and her hand began jacking me in time with her mouth. The onslaught made a tingle spark in my balls and begin to emanate out from there—up my spine and down my cock. Every nerve ending in my body seemed to begin and end where her mouth and hand worked in tandem to bring me release, and I was lost to it. Lost to the sensation of her working me like it was her favorite thing to do and lost to the feelings I was developing for this funny, smart, driven, gorgeous woman who enjoyed being on her knees in front of me.

"Close," I warned, even though I knew it wouldn't slow her down. I knew it because I knew this woman, even though she'd worked hard to make sure I wouldn't. How was it possible two people who knew so little about each other could also know each other so well?

I would've explored that thought more if my brain hadn't whited out as my orgasm barreled down on me. My entire body tensed as my cock pulsed my release into her mouth. She closed her lips around me and continued to suck me through my climax, swallowing my come like she craved it.

My body twitched and shivered as I came down from the high, and she pulled off me with a pop. Her lips looked shiny and red, and it was possibly the most erotic sight I'd ever seen. I reached down and pulled her up, taking her mouth with mine and liking the fact that I could taste myself there.

When we pulled apart because breathing was sadly necessary, she smiled. "Did I help you get over your fears?"

The joke was clear, but the words struck a chord deep within me. Because nothing about what had happened had alleviated any of my fears. If anything, it had ratcheted up all of them.

But there was no way to tell her any of that. This thing between us was convenient and fun and casual. That's what we both wanted, and I'd damned well better remember it. The smart thing would be to pull back and get some distance.

But it had been established long before that I wasn't a smart man. So instead of moving away, I kissed her again and hoped that losing myself in her for a little longer would make me forget how scared I was.

CHAPTER THIRTEEN

ZARA

I figured a blowjob would be just the thing CJ needed to loosen up, but even after our earlier tryst, he'd remained a little tense. He *had* been relaxed enough to return the favor, but where I had been turned into a boneless glob, he'd almost seemed restless as he bounced around the room examining doll parts. He was more himself after returning from a shower.

"Your grandparents have surprisingly good water pressure for a farm. I almost lost an eye when I washed my face."

"It's well water, but I don't know what that means for the pressure."

He hummed but didn't otherwise reply. He only had a towel around his waist, but I was disappointed to see he was wearing boxers underneath when he let the towel drop to the floor so he could get dressed. "So what's the plan for tonight?"

I rolled over in bed where I'd been sprawled on my back and rested my head on my palm. "Those of us who are already here will have dinner. It'll be casual. The big party is tomorrow. But that means you'll likely be the center of everyone's attention tonight."

He waggled his eyebrows. "I don't know if you noticed, but I like being the center of attention."

I giggled but thought of how that didn't seem distinctly

true. In high school, he'd always seemed to like everyone's eyes on him, but that image didn't quite jibe with the man I'd come to know. It wasn't that he came off as opposed to attention, but he didn't seem to revel in it like I always thought he had in school. Maybe he'd changed, or maybe I'd always had a false impression of him.

Either way, I liked the man he'd become—likely more than I should. It was easy to see CJ in my life, even though I was the one who had been more adamant about not wanting anyone in that role right now. But there was no denying I was drawn to him, a feeling that only became stronger the more time we spent together.

"What time do we have to be down there?" he asked.

Looking over at the clock, I saw that it was approaching three. "We should probably head down sooner rather than later and help out. I don't want them to start gossiping about what we're doing up here."

"Would that gossip be inaccurate?" he teased.

"No. But I'd also like it not to be totally obvious."

He laughed. "Hate to break it to you, but it's already totally obvious. We've been up here over an hour."

"We could've been taking a nap."

"Maybe. Hopefully they weren't listening at the door. You're not exactly quiet during your 'naps.'"

I hurried off the bed and stepped in front of him as he looked in the mirror at the cream sweater and dark-gray chinos he'd put on. "And you were?"

"As a mouse," he replied. I would've thought he was being serious if it hadn't been for the twitching of his lips.

"If you say so." I stood there for a moment longer and drank him in. He really was supremely sexy, but my deepening attraction to him was beginning to scare me. He returned my gaze, and I detected a softening in his eyes, which was enough to get me moving. "I'm going to take a quick shower, and then we can head downstairs."

I barely heard him mumble an affirmative as I scooped up my toiletry bag and hightailed it out of the room. It wasn't until I was under the spray that I began to relax. Though relax probably wasn't a great word for it. I was wound too tight, like my skin couldn't quite contain all that was going on inside my body.

I was pretty sure I was falling for Corey Jensen. And what a goddamn mess that was.

COLTON

I didn't know what sent Zara running from the room, but I couldn't help but think it was the same thing that had caused me to hide out in the shower. This...*thing* between us was growing beyond our control. Or maybe just my control. I had no idea how she felt and had no plans to ask. Voicing it out loud would make an already complicated situation even more muddled.

The smart thing to do would be to pull back. Situate us firmly in the friends-with-benefits zone again and make sure we damn well stayed there. But that was a difficult task when we were pretending to be in a relationship.

There wasn't much I could do except keep pretending I was pretending—keep acting like I was into her so we could put on a show for her family and not because I was *actually* into her. For the hundredth time since all this started, I wished I could go back and do everything differently.

If I'd come clean that first night about who I was, we maybe could have seen where this was going to go between us. But as it was, I was fairly certain Zara was going to flay me alive when she found out the truth. Not that I blamed her, but it made being honest with her a little bit more difficult to stomach. And not only because I was afraid of what she'd do to me but because I knew I'd lose her afterward.

Letting out a deep sigh, I gave myself one more look in the mirror. There wasn't anything I could do about any of it this weekend. I'd promised I'd help her out, so that was what I'd focus on. Everything else could be worried about later.

I sat down on the bed and texted Corey that we'd made it up here. His reply came less than a minute later.

Don't do anything I wouldn't do... Like
pretend to be your twin brother and get
dragged into an awkward family reunion.

He really was a dick, and I told him so before shutting off my phone and sliding it into my pocket.

Zara came back into the room and dressed without initiating any conversation. She pulled a long-sleeved blue blouse over her head and turned to me. "Ready?"

"As I'll ever be."

She smiled at that, ran a hand through her hair, and opened the bedroom door. I followed her downstairs, where everyone was milling around. There were a few more family members there than I'd met earlier, so I was introduced to them, and we all made small talk until dinner was ready.

A bell rang behind me, and I jumped, grabbing on to Zara's arm like I was going to have to pull her away from the porcelain doll zombie apocalypse. "What the hell?" I muttered.

There was a tap on my ass that had me spinning around, bringing me face-to-face with Meemaw.

"Just a dinner bell. You need stronger nerves if you're going to make it around here."

My pulse felt like it was going to shoot out of my neck, but I managed a weak smile. "I'll work on strengthening them before the next alarm goes off."

Giving Zara a smirk, she said, "I like him."

Zara threaded her arm through mine. "Me too."

Meemaw nodded and continued on her way into the dining room.

"Sorry about that," Zara said. "I forgot where we were standing."

"In front of Quasimodo's bell tower?"

She laughed. "Such a baby," she muttered as she pulled me into the dining room.

A hodgepodge of dishes, from baked chicken to sausage to mashed potatoes to applesauce, were set up in the center of a long wood table.

"No one wanted to go to a lot of trouble since we have the party tomorrow, so everyone who lives close made something and brought it over," Zara explained.

"Looks amazing." And it did.

"One thing my family can do is cook," she replied.

"So your cooking talent is a genetic gift, huh?" I asked with a teasing lilt in my voice.

Zara shrugged, not appearing to appreciate the joke. "Depends on who you ask."

We looked for two open chairs that were together, and the only ones I saw were near her parents, a fact Zara must have also noticed. She was staring directly at them and took a deep breath and blew it out slowly before moving in that direction.

As we approached them, I realized I'd talked to almost all of Zara's relatives but had only exchanged a few brief words with her immediate family. Was Zara intentionally keeping me at a distance from them, or was it just a coincidence?

Zara slid into a chair beside her mom, and I took the one on Zara's other side. Immediately I was passed a plate of macaroni and cheese, and when I only took a small spoonful, I was yelled at to take more by at least three different family members. These were definitely my kind of people.

"So, CJ," Jane began. "We're so glad you could join us this weekend. Zara never brings anyone to family functions. We're not even sure she's had a boyfriend before." Jane chuckled at her words, but I heard Zara inhale deeply beside me.

"Thank you for inviting me. I'm happy to be here, if for no other reason than to enjoy this amazing food," I said, only half joking.

"Our family always puts on quite the spread," Jane said with a smile.

I gently elbowed Zara in the side. "How come you've never cooked a meal like this for me?" I teased, trying to lighten the mood.

Zara opened her mouth to reply, but her mom's words cut her off. "Don't feel bad, CJ. She's never cooked for us either."

"You've never *let* me cook for you," Zara corrected, her tone acidic.

I'd evidently walked us right into a conversational landmine.

Jane *tsk*ed. "That's nonsense. There's nothing stopping you from inviting us over for a meal. If I didn't take it upon myself to drop in from time to time, I'd never see your place at all." Her mother resumed eating as if her daughter weren't stewing beside her.

Searching for a change in conversation, I turned toward Zara's dad. "Mr. Pierce, Zara tells me you're a fisherman. What do you like to fish for?"

Her dad put his fork down and focused on me, which I took as a good sign. "I enjoy the act of fishing, so the catch isn't overly important to me. But Devon and I took a trip last year to catch tuna. That was a fabulous trip, wasn't it, Devon?"

Zara's brother-in-law looked up, startled, as if he hadn't been expecting anyone to speak to him. "Yes, yes, a great trip, yes," he said as he nodded before resuming eating.

Note to self: stay clear of Devon. I cut my eyes over to Zara and saw her fighting back a laugh, which of course threatened to make me laugh as well.

"Do you fish?" Mr. Pierce asked, which made me realize the flaw in asking him about this topic.

"I don't, actually. My dad took me and my brother a couple of times when we were young, but I haven't been in years."

Mr. Pierce's expression grew tight. It was as if I'd handed him a PETA flier on the harms of recreational fishing. "That's a shame. Your father probably enjoyed taking you boys out. I know I would've if I'd had a son."

And didn't that make me feel like a shitty son. Christ.

"Daughters are capable of fishing," Zara interjected.

"Some daughters, maybe," Mr. Pierce said, his tone clearly conveying that he didn't have two such daughters.

"Fishing looks mind-numbingly boring," Zara's sister said.

"See?" Mr. Pierce asked.

"I would've gone. I'd *still* go. If you ever asked." Zara was pushing food around on her plate as she spoke, and it made me want to teleport us out of there.

"Why do you always need to be asked?" her mom said. "If you want something, say something."

"Fine." Zara looked at her dad. "Next time you go fishing, I'd like to come."

He picked up his fork. "We'll see."

"That was effective," Zara grumbled, but no one responded.

I wanted to shove the mac and cheese in his mouth so he couldn't talk anymore. Reaching under the table, I gave her leg a squeeze. She put her hand over mine and squeezed back.

Not much else was said for the remainder of dinner or dessert, and we made a hasty retreat after the plates had been cleared, claiming exhaustion. Once inside the room, Zara closed the door and leaned back against it. "They drive me crazy."

I hadn't been able to offer much comfort during dinner, but I could now. I walked to her and crowded her against the door. "Want me to make you crazy in a good way?"

She slid her arms around my waist. "God, yes."

So I did.

CHAPTER FOURTEEN

ZARA

"You gonna start running or what?" I turned around to look back at CJ, who was at least fifteen feet behind me. It had been a few years since I'd jogged around my grandparents' land, and I hadn't realized how much I'd missed it.

"What's going on here? You hustle me at the gym that day?"

"Maybe." I smiled, but the joy came more from being here than it did from showing CJ that I wasn't as out of shape as he'd originally thought. Something about being here gave me a renewed energy I hadn't felt in a while. I always loved coming here for Thanksgiving every other year, and though it was winter now, today brought me back. The crisp, fresh air, the leaves crunching under our feet as we ran, the smell of...well, horse shit... It all triggered memories of a simpler time.

With a quick sprint, CJ caught up to me, wrapping his arms around me so I could barely move. His body enveloped mine, making me feel smaller, more vulnerable. He kissed me on the top of my head before releasing me and taking off up the hill toward the houses. "You gonna start running or what?" he called back to me.

"You're such a cheater!"

He turned around and laughed and gave a little shrug.

"If you ain't cheatin', you ain't tryin'." Then he headed for the house and didn't look back until he arrived.

I slowed to a walk a few seconds later for a cooldown. By the time I arrived at the house, CJ was sitting on the porch with a cup of something hot between his hands. "Meemaw made hot chocolate and oatmeal cookies. You want some?"

Not bothering to comment on his use of the name Meemaw, I took a swig from the water bottle I'd left on the porch railing. "We just went for a run. I can't ruin it with cookies. Plus, those oatmeal cookies are usually for the kids."

"They're for anyone who wants a taste," Grandma called from inside the house. How the hell had she even heard us?

"You tell her, Meemaw," CJ yelled back. He was grinning from ear to ear, and I couldn't be sure if it was from the cookie he'd just eaten or the fact that he and Meemaw were somehow besties now.

Unable to resist, I put a hand on his chest and leaned up to kiss him. There was no heat to it—just an innocent peck on the lips that felt more comfortable than sexual.

"What was that for?" he asked, a small smile spreading over his lips after I pulled mine away.

What *was* that for? I gave him a quick shrug. "Gotta keep up appearances."

He wrapped his arms around my waist and pulled me close to him, turning an innocent moment into one that made me hungry for him. I let out a soft groan when he kissed my neck. The salt from his sweat mixed with the subtle scent of his soap created an aroma that was all man—clean and masculine and CJ.

"How much time do we have 'til we have to get ready for the party?" His voice was raspy in my ear, and it did things to me I shouldn't be feeling on my grandparents' porch.

I looked at my watch. "Probably not enough. We both need to get showered and be there in less than two hours."

"I can be fast."

Laughing, I pulled back to look at him. "Such a sweet talker," I joked. "After the party, we'll have all night."

"Is that a promise?"

"It's whatever you want it to be."

COLTON

Once I was showered and shaved, I put on dark jeans, a black T-shirt, and a fitted maroon sweater. I pushed the sleeves up to just below my elbows, rubbed a styling paste between my fingers, and messed with my hair until it sat how I wanted. It was still longer on top, but I'd just gotten it cut before we left, so the sides were clipped short the way I liked.

I felt for the chain around my neck and adjusted it to make sure the clasp was in the back. Then I put on a small amount of cologne—just enough for Zara to smell if she was close—and headed back into our room. "How do I look?"

She was still in her towel, and the thought of what was underneath had me wanting to remove all the clothes I'd just put on—dolls be damned. "Like you should be a model and not an accountant," she answered, her eyes roaming over my body in a way that made me physically feel her gaze.

It was moments like these that made me wonder why I chose to wear fitted jeans around her. They didn't leave much room for my cock to expand, and right now I could feel it doing just that, pressing hard against my pants as it searched for space it wasn't going to find.

"I'm not exactly an accountant," I said, wishing she hadn't interpreted my description of Corey's job that way. I took comfort in the fact that denying the job title was technically the truth. "That makes me sound way nerdier than I am."

"Nerdy's good," she said. "I think it's a turn-on."

"Mmm, well, in that case," I said, bringing a finger to my lips in thought, "I forgot to tell you about my coin collection."

"Oh yeah?" she said, moving closer to me but not close enough for me to touch. "What about it?"

"I have an Indian head penny from 1892."

She licked her lips. "What else?"

I lowered my voice, making it deep and gravelly. "Quarters from every state in the continental US."

"What happened to Alaska and Hawaii?" she asked, taking another step toward me.

"Guess I just never got around to getting them. But one day, I hope to complete the collection."

"So hot," she breathed, and then she bit her lip, pulling on it a bit before finally releasing it.

Clearing my throat, I said, "You should probably get ready so we're on time for the party. I don't want to have to explain what we were doing that made us late to something that's on your grandparents' property. Especially with how long it took us to get down to dinner last night."

She rubbed a hand over my chest and down my abs. "You're very punctual."

"Gotta make a good impression."

She moved close, and we wrapped our arms around each other.

She looked up and smiled. "I think you already have."

CHAPTER FIFTEEN

COLTON

Walking up to the renovated barn, I put a hand on Zara's lower back. "You look beautiful, you know. That dress..." I leaned back a bit to look at her from behind. The fact that it was long-sleeved didn't make it any less sexy. The black-and-white stretchy fabric scooped down to her mid-back and hugged her ass tighter than I would've thought she'd want her family to see.

"What about it?"

"I wanna take it off you."

She laughed and slapped my hand away when it dropped down to her ass. "Well, you'll have to wait until after the party for that, I'm afraid."

"What?" I said, acting surprised. "You mean you don't want me to strip you naked in front of your entire family?"

I chuckled when she seemed to consider it for a minute.

"I'd mind it less than they probably would. And my grandfather hunts, so there are definitely a few guns on the property."

"Noted," I said before pulling open the door for her. I'd never been in a venue like this before, but Zara hadn't been kidding when she'd said the party wasn't in a barn. I mean, technically it was a barn, but it didn't appear that way.

The massive building seemed even larger once inside. The high-vaulted ceilings had wooden crossbeams that matched the dark wood planks of the floor, and there was a second-floor loft space that wrapped around three of the walls so people could look down at the dance floor from above. Against the back wall, there was a small bar that matched the rustic decor of the barn—wood with stone accents.

After seeing the inside, I understood why so many couples chose to rent out the space for their wedding receptions. Not that I'd ever considered what might make a good venue for such an event because I never intended to have a wedding of my own. But I'd been to enough weddings to know what constituted a nice place.

"This place is awesome," I said. "It would make a cool home. I saw something like this on one of those house-flipping shows."

"You like working with your hands, CJ?" a voice asked from behind us.

I turned around to see Zara's dad, and I silently prayed he hadn't heard me talking about getting his daughter naked. "Here and there. If it has an engine, I'm good. I'm not sure any of it would come in handy for house flipping, though."

"You work on cars?" Mr. Pierce asked.

"Motorcycles, actually."

"CJ and his brother own a custom bike shop together."

"Is that right?" Mr. Pierce looked genuinely interested, which saddened me as I remembered I wasn't supposed to know much about the ins and outs of the actual fabrication. When would I learn to think before I spoke? According to Zara, I was the accountant. Images of Zara's dad and grandfather chasing me around the premises with a rifle after lying to their baby girl had my heart skipping beats and me trying to cover my slipup.

"Yeah, CJ Cycles. My brother does most of the actual design and assembly, though. I'm more on the financial side of things."

"I've always wanted to get a bike," Mr. Pierce said. "Maybe we should talk."

Jane, who must've been in earshot, appeared beside her husband and put a hand on her husband's arm. "Or maybe you should give up your deathtrap dream once and for all. You know those things terrify me."

Zara's dad rolled his eyes good-naturedly and sighed. "Happy wife, happy life, I guess," he said with a wink at me and then pointed to the food. "Well, we're headed that way. We'll be at a table by the bar if you want to join us."

"Sure," I said, thankful the conversation hadn't gone further than it did.

Zara introduced me to a few more of her cousins who lived in the area and had just come for the night to go to the party. It was an interesting mix of characters, to say the least. Jane's older brother, Grant, was there with his new wife, Rylie.

"How old is she?" I asked once they were out of earshot. I felt like an asshole for asking, but I had to know.

"She's like six years younger than my cousin Cora, Grant's younger daughter."

"No shit!" I wanted to high-five Grant from across the room, but I did my best to act appalled.

"I know. It's wild. Cora almost lost her shit when she found out her soon-to-be stepmom was only twenty-six. She shouldn't have been surprised, though. No female born before 1994 is named Rylie."

I laughed. "That's so true. I had a dog named Riley, actually. We had to put him down because he started having seizures and walking into walls."

Zara stared at me. "You're fun to bring to a party," she said dryly, and I couldn't help but chuckle.

"Oh, I can be tons of fun," I said, bringing her hands up to my lips and giving them a kiss before swinging her out and then back in again so quickly that she squealed.

"There isn't even any music playing yet."

I grabbed her right hand with my left and put an arm around her waist. "I can sing something," I offered, already beginning the first few lyrics of Van Morrison's "Brown Eyed Girl."

Zara smiled through the first verse but eventually began singing along. We stumbled over a few lines, the lyrics much easier to remember when the actual song was playing. When I got to the chorus, I changed the words to "brown-haired girl" instead. I hadn't intended the song to have a deeper meaning—or a meaning at all, really. I'd just chosen something that I liked and remembered most of, but as I sang, the symbolism of the words hit me hard. Zara and I had gone to school together, grown up together, but we unfortunately hadn't connected until we'd *re*connected. And I was thankful we had.

When we finished singing—a horrendous version that was nowhere close to doing the original justice—I gave Zara a kiss on the forehead before releasing her. "I feel like we should make love in the green grass now," I said, thinking of the image the lyrics conjured.

Her lips turned up into a slow smile before she spoke. "Can we at least wait until it gets a little warmer out?"

"Warmer's probably best. June?"

Her grin widened. "It's a date."

A few minutes later, I met Cora, who, appropriately enough, had brought her fifty-one-year-old boyfriend, Jay. He was a photographer, and they'd met when he'd photographed her naked for a book. It wasn't one of those porno ones, though, Cora had assured us—as if people routinely set porn out in their living rooms for company to peruse at dinner parties. It was an artful collection of real women. I nodded like all of it made sense, and my performance was Oscar-worthy. I was more interested in their golden retriever they'd brought to the party than I was in their weird-ass Woody Allen relationship or the photos of Cora's sideboob that Jay thrust in our faces.

"He's older than Grant by four months," Zara said when they were gone.

"They brought their dog," I said slowly, "to an anniversary party."

Zara burst out laughing. "They're weird. In case you haven't noticed."

"You don't say?"

"I guess I'm just used to it. My family's a little different. Sorry if this is all...a little much." Zara looked apologetic.

"Don't look at me like that. Your eyes look like Cora and Jay's dog's."

"Thanks," Zara said with a laugh.

"I didn't mean it like that. I meant... It's me who should be sorry. I put you in an awkward spot when I said I'd come to this with you."

"No, you didn't." She grabbed my hands in hers and held them there. "I could've said no. Made up an excuse for why you couldn't have come."

"So why didn't you?" I asked, genuinely curious.

She shrugged. "Because I want you here with me."

"I want to be here too." And it felt good to tell the truth.

ZARA

Somehow CJ held his own with my family for the majority of the night. He ate the seconds and thirds my grandmother insisted he eat because he looked like he needed "some meat on his bones," and he spent a good half hour dancing with my cousins' kids—the oldest of whom was eight.

Seeing CJ on the dance floor spinning around with toddlers and elementary schoolers gave me a new appreciation for the goofball, who was really just a big kid himself. The children looked like they were having the time of their lives when he tried to breakdance and do the worm—a move I especially enjoyed because it looked more like he was humping the floor.

He took a break to get some water and was sitting for just a few minutes before my cousin's twelve-year-old son, Charlie, came running over.

"You know any *Fortnite* dances?"

CJ raised an eyebrow at me and then looked back to Charlie. "Nope, but I have a feeling I'm about to learn some." Then he headed back out and spent the next twenty minutes or so acting like a complete fool and loving every minute of it. I pretended not to notice when he motioned for me to join him, but he was relentless, finally coming over and pulling me out of my chair. "I'm gonna teach you the Fresh," he said. "Charlie told me I'm catching on quick and I should start a YouTube channel."

"I don't think you need a YouTube channel."

He was swinging his arms like Carlton on *Fresh Prince* as he spoke. "Fine. *We* can start a YouTube channel."

"And what makes you think I'm interested in starting a YouTube channel with you?"

He grabbed my hands and swung my arms out and back in again before spinning me around. "We're good together, don't you think?"

I tried not to read into his words because, after all, that's all they were. We'd spent a lot of time here putting on an act, pretending we were something we weren't. Sometimes I got so wrapped up in the story line, I forgot it was only a performance.

But somehow during the last twenty-four hours or so, the lines between fiction and reality had become so blurry I could barely make them out anymore. Our feelings for each other seemed real. They were evident in the small, innocent touches we shared in front of my family as much as they were during the privacy of our own room when no one was there to watch.

"We *are* good together," I agreed as I moved close to him. "Great, actually."

A grin spread wide across his face before he brought his lips toward mine and gave me a soft kiss.

I had to remind myself not to deepen the kiss—not to give in to the near-constant desire I had for this man—but the need to be as close to him as possible was overwhelming. I felt like I could drown in it if I didn't remember to stop and come up for oxygen.

He hovered his lips over mine and barely grazed them before pulling away and dancing like a lunatic again.

I couldn't take my eyes off him.

CHAPTER SIXTEEN

ZARA

The next morning was a lazy one, consisting of pancakes, coffee, and quiet conversations in my grandparents' kitchen, where my family attempted to find out everything they could about CJ before we left because they were scared they might never see him again. It wasn't going to be easy to tell them we broke up when the time came.

My parents would be especially devastated, as my dad already seemed to be thinking of CJ as the son he'd always wished for. Not that my brother-in-law wasn't a good guy. He was. But CJ and my dad had found some sort of connection over all things stereotypical male: sports, motorcycles, household projects. And he had just invited him on his next fishing trip.

"I said *I* would go," I nearly whined, sounding more annoyed than I actually was. I couldn't help but enjoy the fact that my parents seemed invested in CJ, even if their investment would end up being as worthless as a stock on Black Tuesday.

My dad shrugged. "I already have a partner," he said, putting a hand on CJ's shoulder. "Maybe next time."

CJ looked at me apologetically, like it was his fault my dad had chosen him over me. "Or we could all go together," he suggested, to which my dad laughed loudly, effectively grounding the idea before it even had a chance to take flight.

And to further squash it, he said, "That'd be a little awkward, don't you think?"

Not any more awkward than taking your daughter's fake boyfriend on a male-bonding adventure.

"I guess," I said. Knowing the fishing trip would never come to fruition, guilt flooded me quicker than it had all weekend. I'd never liked lying to my parents, and this weekend had been a true test of my ability to withstand my own conscience.

I looked at CJ, who'd just tried to grab another slice of bacon off the fresh pile on a plate next to my grandmother's stove.

She swatted his hand away. "Hold your horses. You'll burn yourself."

CJ chuckled and slowly put his fingers on a strip of the breakfast meat before lifting it to his mouth and taking a bite. "I survived," he said after swallowing. "The reward's worth the risk. You really know how to cook bacon, Meemaw."

My grandmother grinned so widely, I thought I noticed some wrinkles around her eyes and mouth that hadn't been there before. "And you really know how to sweet-talk an old lady."

Leaning back in his chair with a sternness I rarely saw on him, my grandfather scolded CJ with his eyes from the kitchen table. "Better watch it, young man. She's taken."

CJ held up his hands—one still holding the slice of bacon. "I'd never dream of it. Besides, I got a girl." He reached an arm around my waist and leaned down to kiss me on the temple. "And I don't plan on letting go of her anytime soon."

I knew the comment was for show, but I smiled anyway because hearing those words filled me with a warmth I didn't want to lose. But I knew I had no choice. We'd be leaving soon, and things would go back to how they'd been when most of what we'd seen of each other had been without clothes on. It wasn't that I didn't like that—I freakin' *loved* it—but this, what we had here...well, I liked that too.

I just had to find a way to go back to normal. Whatever normal looked like now.

COLTON

The ride home seemed to go fast. Too fast, actually. I probably should have stayed awake for more of it so I could have fully appreciated the last few hours of our weekend together. Groggy, I checked the clock on Zara's dash, which told me we would be home in about forty-five minutes.

She wasn't aware I'd woken up, so I took the opportunity to watch her. To study every beautiful feature—the light freckles on her nose and part of her cheeks that seemed to darken in the sunlight, her strands of soft blond hair that she'd swept behind her ear to expose her neck, where I could swear I could see her pulse beating.

I wanted to kiss her there, feel the evidence of her heart beating against my lips. Her eyes were hidden by dark sunglasses, and I wondered what she was thinking about. I could sometimes tell what she was thinking—or feeling—by the look in her eyes. I wanted to know what she was thinking now more than ever.

Reaching a hand over to place on hers, I said, "Are we there yet?"

She looked over at me, my head resting on the back of the seat as I watched her. "When did you get up, sleepyhead?"

"A few minutes ago."

Laughing, she shook her head. "You were just staring at me, weren't you?"

"Possibly. Does it bother you?"

She thought for a moment before answering. "No. It doesn't. I like that you like to look at me."

"Good. Because I don't really have any plans to stop it anytime soon."

She didn't respond, and I felt a pang of anxiety. "Hey," I said, and I waited until she looked at me again. "You okay? What are you thinking about?" I wasn't sure I wanted to know the answer, but I couldn't help but ask the question anyway. Despite all the lies that had transpired since we'd reconnected, I needed the truth to be present wherever it could.

"The restaurant, actually."

I squeezed her hand in mine. "What about it?"

"Will it be weird for you? If I buy it, I mean?" The thin line of her lips told me this question hadn't occurred to her just now. It was probably something she'd been wondering about for some time.

"No. Why would it be weird?"

"I don't know. Well, I do, but I don't know how to verbalize it." She slid her sunglasses up to the top of her head, pushing her hair back.

"Try."

She ran her free hand over the steering wheel while she thought. "It feels like I'm taking something that's yours."

"You aren't *taking* something. And it isn't mine."

"It's your family's," she said. "Your mom's. And she's not even here to agree to it. I don't know. When I first considered buying it, we didn't have...whatever we have now. I guess it just feels more personal than it should."

"It is more personal." Zara seemed to tense at my words, so I put a hand on her shoulder and massaged it gently. "But not in a bad way. I'm not gonna lie. It's hard to see the restaurant go. There's a part of me at that place, a part of my mom...of all of us. But I can't imagine my dad selling it to just anyone."

"Maybe he shouldn't sell it at all," she suggested.

"He can't afford it, Zara. If he could, he'd keep it. He can't make the repairs anymore or run the place on his own. It's too much. And Co—my brother and I aren't close enough to help him."

Sighing, she said, "I guess you're right."

"As much as I love being right, I wish I weren't right about this. But I know how hard it's been on him, and I know he's given this a lot of thought. I want to support him in that." I brought her hand up and gave it a soft kiss. "And I want to support you too."

"Thanks," she said. "That means a lot."

That's what I was afraid of.

CHAPTER SEVENTEEN

COLTON

Zara and I hung out a few times after we got back from her grandparents' party, and things between us had only grown more intense. We saw more of each other—naked, of course—and Zara was becoming increasingly difficult for me to resist. Somehow we'd transitioned from our purely physical relationship to one that seemed like something more, though I didn't know what *exactly* more was. Other than some Netflix or grabbing a bite to eat or whatever.

I wondered if Zara had noticed the shift, but I didn't want to bring it up, mainly because I didn't want to analyze what it meant. Especially if it didn't mean anything. Which it probably didn't.

After being constantly in each other's company for a weekend, it felt normal to spend time together, and I didn't want to read more into things than were necessary, especially when this would inevitably end. There was no building something whose foundation was a lie. And I reminded myself I didn't want to anyway.

I was getting dressed to meet her at a Korean place she wanted to try when Corey came in.

"What are you up to?" he asked.

"Nothing much. Just meeting Zara for dinner."

When he didn't respond, I turned to look at him and saw him staring at me smugly. "What?" I asked.

He shrugged. "Just didn't think I'd ever see the day."

"Thursday?"

"No, dipshit. The day you, the self-proclaimed bachelor for life, would be dating someone."

I stiffened. "We're not dating."

Corey narrowed his eyes at me. "What do you call it?"

"Hanging out."

"Hanging out? Really? Are we back in high school?"

I walked over to my bed, grabbed my sweater, and pulled it on. "What would you call it, then?"

"I already told you. I call it dating."

"And I already told *you* that we're not dating."

He seemed to think for a second. "So you're banging other people, then?"

"No."

"Is she?"

The thought alone made my stomach hurt, but Corey didn't need to know that. "Not that I know of," I bit out.

"But you are still having sex with each other?" When I rolled my eyes at him, he continued. "So you're exclusively having sex with each other, and on top of that, you're meeting for meals and...whatever else you two do when you're not naked."

"Do you have a point in all this?"

He crossed his arms over his chest and smiled. "Define dating for me, Colt."

"You're such a pain in the ass," I grumbled, but he looked like he was willing to wait me out, so I answered him. "It's when two people commit to be boring with only each other.

And we're anything but boring."

He scoffed. "Yeah, because sitting on someone's couch watching serial killer documentaries is so thrilling."

Why did I ever tell him anything? It always came back to haunt me.

"We haven't established that we're not seeing other people. We just happen to not be."

"Semantics. You may not have discussed it, but you've both obviously mentally made the decision to only see each other."

"I don't know that she's made that decision."

"So you're admitting that you have?" Christ, he looked proud of himself.

"I don't need to play the field when I have a sure thing lined up already," I said, even though the words tasted bitter in my mouth. Truth was, sleeping with someone else didn't hold any appeal. I couldn't remember the last time I'd even *looked* at another woman with any intent behind it.

Holy fuck, was I dating?

No. Dating was something both parties agreed on. There was a conversation and flowers and hugging and it was romantic and not like anything that had happened between Zara and me.

He stood there staring and smiling at me like the freak he was, so I moved past him. "Just because you haven't seen any action in a while doesn't mean you get to give me a hard time for having a sex life. I gotta go."

"Okay," he yelled down the hall after me. "Enjoy your *date*."

I let the door slam shut behind me and didn't even consider locking it. Hopefully someone would murder him while I was gone.

ZARA

I waited in the lobby of the restaurant for CJ. He'd offered to pick me up, but I was already downtown, so it made more sense to meet here. Even though I kind of cursed the fact that we'd have two cars. I was fairly certain he'd come back to my place after dinner, but I would've liked to have removed all other options.

A moment later, a gust of cold air swirled around me as the door opened. Looking up, I saw CJ enter, hunkered down into his coat against the freezing temperatures. When he looked up and saw me, he made his way over and bent down to give me a quick kiss. As he straightened, an odd look came over his face, as if he'd been thrown by his own action—which was strange because he'd greeted me that way every time he'd seen me since we'd returned from my grandparents' house.

"You okay?" I asked him.

He shook his head as if clearing it. "Yeah, yeah, I'm good, yeah."

I almost called him out for sounding like Devon, but he didn't look like he was up for being teased. There was a tension in his posture and a strain evident on his face that put me on alert.

"Hungry?" I asked, trying to steer us away from the awkwardness that seemed to shroud us.

"Starving." He said it with a smile that looked genuine and made me feel a little more at ease.

We made our way to the hostess stand, checked in for our reservation, and were shown to our seats immediately. CJ pulled out my chair before sitting across from me, and we each took a minute to look over the menus. A server quickly came to fill our water glasses, inform us of the specials, and take our drink order before hurrying away.

"The shrimp special sounded good," I said as I picked up my water to take a sip.

"My brother thinks we're dating."

His words startled me, causing me to gulp the water and choke. Grabbing my napkin, I covered my mouth and coughed into it a few times before looking up at CJ.

His eyes were wide, as if he couldn't believe he'd said the words out loud. "I maybe could've said that with more tact."

"Maybe just a bit. Now what are you talking about?"

"He came in while I was getting ready and said it was nice to see me dating."

"But we're not dating."

"That's what I told him. But he went on and on about how if we were hanging out all the time and weren't sleeping with anyone else, then that was basically dating. And I told him that I didn't even know if we were sleeping with only each other. I mean, *I'm* only having sex with you, but I couldn't speak for you. Not that I'm accusing you of banging a ton of guys, but we haven't talked about it, so you could be. And that would be fine. Totally fine."

He didn't look like that would be fine, and damn if that didn't warm my insides. "CJ," I interrupted, even though I kind of hated to because a flustered and rambling CJ was a sight to behold. "I'm not sleeping with anyone else."

"Okay. Good. That's good. Me neither."

I'd gotten that message already but didn't point it out. "That doesn't mean we're dating, though." I hesitated for a second. "Does it?"

We stared at each other for a pregnant moment before

the server came back and broke our staring contest. After both grappling awkwardly for our menus, the server asked if we wanted him to come back in a few more minutes. But before he left, he said, "I forgot we also have a beef special for two. It's popular with couples."

He went on to describe how it was prepared, but I'd tuned him out. Because while I wasn't stupid and therefore wasn't under any delusions that CJ and I were just buddies, it truly hadn't hit me that other people looked at us as though we were in a relationship. Which, okay, maybe that did make me stupid. A man and woman out at dinner together screamed romantically involved. But what maybe threw me more than people thinking that about us was that it seemed...accurate. Or maybe I just *wanted* it to be.

I knew I had feelings for him. I'd mentally owned up to them over a week ago. But saying them out loud was daunting, especially since I'd told him time and again that this was just sex. Somewhere along the way, mixed signals had become my language, and I wasn't sure how to set the record straight.

Looking up at him after the server left us, I let myself get lost in his eyes and imagined life without him. It made my chest ache. "I think we're dating," I blurted out.

He took a deep breath that made me concerned about the words that would leave his mouth when he exhaled. But then he smiled, and just like that, I knew it would be all right.

"I think so too. My brother is never going to let me live this down."

We laughed, and then as if by some unspoken agreement, we picked up our menus. I felt like we should have more to say on the matter, but we just...didn't. We'd fallen into this change in our relationship status much like we'd fallen into every other aspect of it—completely by accident.

Even though I'd never felt like I'd had more purpose in my life.

CHAPTER EIGHTEEN

COLTON

"How much snow are we supposed to get tonight?" I pulled Zara's blinds up a bit to look outside. "It's coming down pretty heavy." I'd spent the majority of the day here, and though I knew it was supposed to snow, I hadn't checked the weather since yesterday morning.

"It said we could get up to eight inches before it's done."

I nodded as I thought about how dating someone who lived forty-five minutes from where I worked and lived could be more problematic than I'd anticipated. The snow would be enough to weigh down power lines, enough to cover Zara's whole car and the ground around it. I wanted to be here with her—keep her warm if the electricity went out, shovel out her car in the morning after we slept in and had breakfast. And if I left tonight, it might take me hours to get home, and I had work in the morning.

This was the kind of bullshit decision-making I wanted nothing to do with. I hated how I'd have to consider the impact of my choices on someone else. Not because I didn't care about Zara or about her life. I did. I wanted to know about her family and her interests and what she had for breakfast. I wanted to know all of it. But having my life so closely linked to another person's was a lot of responsibility—especially with someone

I felt so much for.

"You still wanna go out to eat? We can order something if it's easier." I felt her arms slip around me as I looked at snow covering her lawn. "Or I could cook."

We had plans to go to a nice sushi restaurant in the city and then to see one of Zara's friends sing at some sort of open mic thing we'd promised we'd go to. "What about Miranda's thing?"

"She'll survive," she said simply. "She goes to them all the time. I went to one two weeks ago."

"Oh." I could hear the surprise in my voice. "Why didn't you invite me then?"

I felt her shrug. I turned to face her and slid my arms around her too.

"We weren't serious then," she said. "I guess hearing Miranda's drunken version of Adele's 'When We Were Young' isn't my idea of foreplay."

I burst out with a laugh. "Well, now I want to go more than ever."

"Believe me, there's nothing hot about any of it. One time she threw up right as she sang the last line."

"That's...gross."

Zara nodded slowly, like she was still traumatized from the memory. "The open mic was closed after that."

Both of us tried to hold in laughs that eventually escaped. "Okay, so we'll give Miranda a rain check. Or a snow check, I guess I should say. But we can still go get dinner. We have reservations, and I'm sure we'll be finished eating before it gets too bad out."

Zara thought for a moment. "You know what? Neither of us have even gotten in the shower yet. Let's just stay here. I'll make something for us, and we can find something to do here."

Raising an eyebrow, I said, "I have an idea."

"We already did that twice today," she teased. "Three for me, actually."

"Not that," I said. "Well, we can still do that. But I was actually thinking we could go sledding."

"Where? On what? Childless adult women aren't normally known for their selection of winter toys."

"Anything can be used as a sled," I said, shocked that she'd never gone down a hill on a trash can lid. "Didn't you ever make an impromptu sled in high school if it started snowing while you were out?"

"I feel like I should just lie and say yes."

"Oh, no. No lying." The words stung on my tongue as I said them, and if I'd been able to filter them before they'd come out, I would've. But my excitement at the prospect of doing something I hadn't done in years got the best of me, and as usual, my mouth moved quicker than my brain. "If I'm going to take your household item sledding virginity, I need some advance notice." I lowered my voice to a deep rasp that I hoped would sound sexy. "It's gonna feel so good."

She bit back a smile. "What are we going to do it on?"

"What do you have? Air mattress? Laundry basket? Cookie sheet greased with PAM?"

"Who's Pam?" she asked, her face so serious, it made the comment even funnier. "I thought I wasn't sharing you."

I gave her a swat on her ass and then slid my hand into the back pocket of her jeans. I brought my other hand up to rub the back of her head, playing with her hair between my fingers. "You don't. I'm all yours."

And better yet, she was all mine. For now, at least.

ZARA

I pulled my hat down over my ears before brushing off whatever snow I could from my pants. Before going outside, we'd gotten as bundled up as we could—luckily I'd gone skiing a few years ago, so I at least had some waterproof pants. But CJ, poor guy, was wearing only his jeans, which, from the looks of them, were so frozen I was worried they might actually crack and fall off him. At least he'd had boots in his car.

"We can go back whenever you want," I offered, though the kid in me was secretly hoping he'd hang for the long haul.

"I'm good. I forgot how much fun it is to sled on a golf course."

"Until we get arrested."

He grabbed the twin air mattress, and we headed up to the top of the hill. Even though we'd decided to go out before dinner so it wouldn't be as cold and dark, we'd already been sledding at least an hour, and the only light to be seen was the reflection of the moon on the snow—which was still falling, though not as heavily. "We won't get arrested. No cops are worried about two old people playing in the snow."

"We aren't old." I looked at him for confirmation. "Are we?"

"I'm not sure. I don't *feel* old. But most of my friends are married, and some have kids."

"Mine too."

"That doesn't mean we're old, though. We just took a different path, that's all."

"A path that involves wine, trespassing, and numb fingers," he said, rubbing his hands together and blowing into them.

"Definitely the better option," I said. "I still think you

should've worn a pair of my leggings under your jeans."

"If I freeze to death tonight, I can't have my family wondering if I was about to go all Caitlyn Jenner on them."

As he positioned the air mattress so we weren't going to head toward the small pond on the eighth hole, I thought about what we'd just talked about. It was a point I didn't often labor over, though it was true nonetheless. I didn't exactly want kids—I never really had—but I didn't *not* want them either. I'd just never been at a place in my life where I could picture caring about someone else as much, if not more, than I did myself.

Until I'd reconnected with CJ, that is. I found myself falling for him in a way that I tried to deny. We'd had an instant attraction that, on my part at least, had been present in high school. But what I'd felt then, what I felt *currently* was more than just satisfying a childhood crush. And once we'd both allowed ourselves to acknowledge our real feelings, we'd gotten closer than I'd anticipated more quickly than I'd expected.

He held a hand out to help me sit down in front of him.

I let him pull me between his legs and wrap his arms around me. "They'd never think that. I doubt the morgue would tell them what you were wearing."

He squeezed my sides in an attempt to tickle me, but thankfully my coat was a thick enough defense. "Okay, two more times, and then we'll head back. I've worked up an appetite. Ready?"

Before I could respond, we were flying down the hill. Like every other time, the mattress was all over the place because it had two grown adults on it and no handles or other means of steering.

Our breaths came out in loud puffs as we laughed after CJ somehow fell off the back. I went about fifteen feet more before I came to a complete stop. I lay on the mattress for a few moments, looking up at the falling snow.

"Make room for me!" CJ yelled. Before I could react, he flopped down next to me, his weight popping the mattress at the seam. "Oops," he said as we slowly deflated all the way down to the snow. "I'll buy you a new one."

"Don't worry about it. I haven't used this thing since I moved out of my one-bedroom a few years ago."

"What are we gonna sled on next time it snows?" He asked the question like it made all the sense in the world.

I rolled my head to the side so I could see him. Then I gave him a soft kiss. His lips were somehow still warm enough to make me want them on other parts of me. "I guess we'll just have to invest in a two-person sled."

"Buying a sled together, huh? That's a serious step. It's like...three steps away from a puppy."

"I think it's at least four or five 'til we're in puppy territory," I assured him.

This time he turned to look at me. "Okay," he said. "What color do you want?"

"White with one of those brown spots around its eye." I let the silence hover above us. "Kidding. I like red."

He smiled and rolled onto his side to bring a snowy, gloved hand to my face. "Me too."

CHAPTER NINETEEN

COLTON

I pulled up in front of Zara's town house and idled for a second, wondering if doing this in person was the best way to go about this. Though I figured there really was no *best* way to go about it.

The better things got with Zara, the worse I felt, because there was no way around it: I was going to lose her. No scenario I conjured in my mind resulted in a happy ending for us.

But wasn't that how things always worked out? Happy endings were for fairy tales and romcoms. Even my parents, who'd loved more deeply than any two people I'd ever seen, hadn't gotten the ending they deserved. Instead, my dad watched his wife waste away in bed as she writhed in pain from the disease that was eating her from the inside out.

He'd been her rock through it all, but I wasn't that guy. I wasn't one to settle down and go all-in. Even if Zara had made me believe for a little while that I could be. Because my feelings for her were real, and if there was any way I could've told her the truth and kept her, I would have. If I could go back to the night of the reunion and been honest from the jump, I would.

Though that likely would have meant never getting to know her in the first place, since she'd made it clear she wasn't fond of who I really was. But maybe that would've been for the best, because the path we were on now was headed to crash and burn. I'd been a dick keeping the truth from her, and she was likely going to begin plotting my death as soon as I told her, which I deserved. I deserved a lot of things: her ire, her harsh words, her hatred.

I just wished I deserved *her*. But I didn't, and it was time to come clean about that. I'd already waited almost two months to be honest. The least I could do was face her wrath head-on.

I climbed out of my car and made my way to her door. I'd texted earlier to say I was heading over, and she'd told me she'd leave the door open. Which wasn't the safest thing for her to do, but I didn't feel like I was in the position to lecture her about it. I walked into her home and looked around. I could've seen myself spending a lot more time here if I hadn't been a lying prick who was about to get tossed on his ass.

"Zar? I'm here."

"I'll be right down," she yelled. "Or you could come up." The flirty invitation was clear, but there was no way I would take her up on it.

"I'm going to grab a drink of water."

"Okay," she yelled back, dragging out the initial vowel.

I wandered into the kitchen and grabbed a bottle of water from the fridge and toyed with it while I waited. Maybe the kitchen wasn't the best place to have this discussion. Too many knives. But a change of venue was out of the question as she bounced into the room, immediately coming over to me to give me a kiss—which I allowed myself to soak up since I was sure it would be the last one I ever received from her—and then went to grab herself a drink.

"So what do you want to do tonight? I could go for takeout

from that pub around the corner."

When I didn't answer her, she looked up. "You okay?"

"Yeah." My voice was raspy, as if it had been scrubbed with a Brillo pad. I cleared my throat and tried again. "Yeah, I'm fine. But...I need to talk to you about something."

She moved closer to me and crossed her arms over her chest. "What is it?"

"It's... I need to... Fuck, this is hard..." I scrubbed a hand over my face.

"Is this about the restaurant? Because I think your dad and I have come to an agreement that'll make everyone happy."

I put up a hand to cut her off. "No, it's not that. But I'm glad you've figured it out." And I hoped what I said next didn't fuck it all up.

She moved closer and rested a hand on my arm. "Then what is it?"

The concern on her face nearly killed me. How could I have done this to her? To us? I was such a fucking asshole.

When I didn't respond, she continued. "Are you okay? You're freaking me out a little here."

I laughed humorlessly. "Nothing about me is okay."

"What the hell is going on? Out with it, Corey."

Corey. It was a name she'd barely used since that first night, and it let me know just how scared and frustrated she must be to use it after all this time. The lack of hearing it had made it easy to ignore the truth. But this was the reality I'd carved for us: one where I loved a woman who didn't even know who I was.

My gaze fell to the counter in front of me. "I'm not Corey," I said quietly. But she deserved better than that, so I lifted my head and owned the fraud I'd allowed myself to become—the lie I'd allowed her to believe. "I'm not Corey." My voice was strong and clear, even though I didn't feel either of those things.

She withdrew her hand from me and stepped back as if I'd electrocuted her. And maybe I had. I'd electrocuted our entire relationship in three words, and there wasn't a damn thing I could do to revive it. We were DOA, and even though I'd known how this would end from the beginning, tears still pricked my eyes and my throat convulsed. But I wasn't the one who had a right to be upset in this scenario, so I forced myself to remain strong.

For once, I'd face her as the man I was, not the one she thought I was.

ZARA

"What?" was the only word I could force out. My lungs felt like they were constricting, and I had an errant thought that I might be in the beginning stages of a panic attack.

"I'm so sorry" was all he said. He as in...Colton? How was this happening?

"You're sorry? Are you fucking kidding me right now?" I turned away and pushed my hands through my hair.

He rushed to explain. "You said you knew who I was, and by the time I realized you thought I was Corey, we'd already...you know." He gestured with his hands, as if saying the words was somehow the most uncomfortable part of this conversation. "And then when I saw you the next time, I tried to tell you, but you kept saying we didn't need to talk, and then—"

Rounding on him, I planted my hands on my hips. "So this is *my* fault?"

His hands shot out in front of him. "No, no, absolutely not.

I one hundred percent know this is completely my fault. I had thousands of opportunities to tell you, but in the beginning, I wasn't sure it even mattered because it was so casual. But then all these feelings started, and it got harder and harder to be honest."

"It should never be hard to be honest. Not about something as fundamental as your goddamn name."

His face contorted. "Never hard to be honest? Do you hear yourself right now?"

"What the hell is that supposed to mean?"

"Nothing. That... I shouldn't have said that."

"No, you don't get to be a chickenshit right now. Tell me what you meant."

"It's just that... I mean, you're not exactly a paragon of honesty. We lied to your entire family for a whole weekend."

Pointing a finger at him, I noticed my hands were shaking. Whether it was from anger or sadness, I didn't know. "*You* got us into that mess, just like you got us into this one."

He sighed and seemed to deflate in front of me. "I'm just saying neither of us is a stranger to lying. And I get that mine was infinitely worse. I own every bit of that. But I didn't intentionally mislead you. You said you could always tell us apart. Why would I doubt that?"

"You want to know why I thought you were Corey?"

He didn't answer.

"Because you were a complete punk in high school. Conceited and arrogant. And the man I saw at the reunion didn't exude any of that. But I see it now. You've just gotten better at hiding it over the years."

"That's not who I am. That's not who I've ever been. You didn't even know me in high school, but you made a whole host of judgments anyway."

"So I deserve this?" I wanted to kill him. I'd never felt more capable of it.

"No. You don't deserve any of this. But I didn't let it go this far to hurt you. In my own stupid way, I was trying to keep you. I knew once I told you the truth, I'd lose you. And I let my fear of that override doing the right thing. And I'm so, so sorry for that. I'd do anything to take it back."

So would I. I'd do anything to be able to go back and have us both make different choices. I hadn't been sure I was talking to Corey that night. I'd taken a guess that I'd thought had ended up being a lucky one. But he'd made the choice to keep going with the lie. He'd made me fall in love with someone he wasn't. And that...that was an egregious mistruth I couldn't even wrap my brain around. "I don't even know what to say."

He shoved his hands into the pockets of the jacket he'd never even bothered to remove. "I get that. I wouldn't have much to say to me either if I were you."

We stood in my kitchen, studiously avoiding making eye contact for what felt like hours.

"I guess—" He cleared his throat before starting again. "I guess this is it."

I guessed it was too, but I didn't say the words. I didn't say anything. I just watched the man I was falling in love with apologize one more time before walking out of my kitchen, out of my house, and out of my life.

It was surreal. That one minute something could be rock solid and the next it could be gone. That something I'd counted on never truly existed at all.

But the worst part was that the person who'd made me feel things I'd never felt before, who'd claimed to have felt those things too, could just...leave. I wasn't sure I could've ever gotten past the lie, but that didn't matter. Colton hadn't even given me a chance to decide what I could live with and what I couldn't. What I could forgive and what I couldn't get past. He'd just fucking *left*.

He hadn't fought for me. And that said more about the kind of man he was than anything else.

I looked around my kitchen, took in how empty it was, and let the tears that had been building fall. For all the things that would never be, and worse—for all the things that never really had been. When I was finally able to pull myself together, I grabbed my phone, deleted my entry for CJ, and told myself I'd be able to delete him from my heart just as quickly.

Colton had lied to me easily enough. What harm could there be in lying to myself?

CHAPTER TWENTY

ZARA

I wasn't sure why I always cooked when I was stressed. Even though I enjoy cooking, it only created a mess I eventually had to clean up. And cleaning was *not* something I enjoyed. Which made the fact that my kitchen was speckled in homemade gravy and flour from handmade raviolis all the more depressing. I cooked to distract myself. I cooked because there was some kind of catharsis to it that I couldn't describe. Or at least that was usually the case.

Though I couldn't say I'd ever used it as a way to take my mind off a devastating breakup. Cooking clearly didn't have the same effect on my mental state as it did when I used it as a way to procrastinate before studying for a test in college or after a fight with my sister in high school.

It'd been a few days since CJ—Colton—had told me the truth, and it hadn't gotten any easier. Not that I felt like it really should have. Every day felt like I was mourning the loss of someone I'd never even known to begin with.

All I could hope was that time and distractions would make things better. But since I didn't have a job that took up the majority of my time, all I had to take my mind off CJ/Corey/Colton was the restaurant venture, which now seemed more awkward than ever. Though I hoped it would be more awkward for him than for me.

My cell phone rang, and I could see it was Becca calling. We usually did a pretty good job of talking to each other at least once a week, but I hadn't spoken to her in a few weeks because she'd been away for work. She was no doubt calling in response to the text I'd sent her about CJ. I tapped the phone with my knuckle and told her to hold on a second while I washed my hands.

"Don't tell me to hold on after you send a text like that!" I heard her say even though the phone wasn't on speaker.

"Sorry. I was cooking," I said, putting the phone to my ear. "How was Detroit?"

"Cold, and I didn't see Eminem anywhere, so it's not worth talking about. Now tell me what's going on."

"I already did."

"No. I mean what's happening *now*?"

"I'm avoiding him and all thoughts associated with him." I grabbed some disinfectant wipes and began scrubbing the countertop like I was cleaning up after a murder. Come to think of it, I was surprised there hadn't been one when he'd finally come clean.

"That seems healthy," Becca said.

"Better than the alternative."

"Which is what?"

I hadn't really considered any specific answer to this question until Becca asked it. "I don't know. Thinking about him. Talking to him. Which I'm definitely *not* about to do. It's bad enough I'll have to see him with this whole restaurant thing happening. You know how bad I am at awkward encounters."

"Guess you'll have to get better at it unless you want to retract your offer."

There was absolutely no way I would let that happen. "That's not even an option I'm willing to entertain. This isn't my fault. *He* can be the one who feels like the asshole. Not me."

"I'm sure he does feel like an asshole," she said, her voice way too sympathetic for my liking.

"You're not defending him, are you?"

"No. I'm not defending him. He impersonated someone he isn't. It's inexcusable, Zar. Even if you made the mistake initially, he had a million opportunities to tell you who he really was."

"Yeah, well...I know who he really is now."

COLTON

"Can you toss me the tape when you're done with it?" asked Corey. "My roll just ran out."

I finished dragging out the piece I had in my hand so the blue tape hit perfectly at the edge of the ceiling. "Here," I said, not even waiting until he was ready before I chucked the tape in his direction across the room.

"What the hell's your problem?"

"Nothing. I was just trying to balance on the ladder as I threw it."

He lifted his left eyebrow in a way that I couldn't and I'd secretly always been a little envious of. "You've been irritable for days."

I climbed down off the ladder and went to grab a paintbrush so I could start cutting in the edges of the walls. "I'm PMSing."

Corey barked out a laugh, but he didn't actually sound amused. Truth was, I knew I'd been an asshole, but there wasn't much I could do to change it. I felt like Bruce Banner stuck in perpetual Hulk form. "Whatever. You'll tell me eventually."

I actually wasn't sure I would, because my fuckup was more epic than hurting Zara. Corey'd warned me that I might screw over our family in the process, and I wasn't about to share that news, especially here in the restaurant when I was supposed to be helping Dad, not hurting him. "Who picked this paint color? Dad doesn't strike me as a dark purple kind of guy."

Corey groaned something unintelligible that probably meant he had no clue who'd picked it. "Maybe Zara." He said it like it made all the sense in the world, because how would he know otherwise?

I laughed harshly. "I highly doubt that."

I felt Corey walk toward me more than saw him. It was one of those telepathic twin connections that was impossible to explain unless you *were* a twin. "What did you do?"

When I turned toward him, he was standing directly in front of me, his arms crossed in a way that made me think he was more disappointed than angry. It only made me feel worse than I already did. "What do you think?"

His eyes bored into mine for a silent moment that was filled with more emotion than any words could convey. I stood to meet his stare, and to avoid the tears that would inevitably find their way behind my eyes if I looked at him long enough, I said, "I don't need your shit too. I heard enough from her."

"God, you're such a moron."

"Thanks, Cor. That's exactly what I need."

He pulled at his hair before letting his hands run down his face. "Did you ever think about what Dad needed?"

I felt my voice rising with my anger before I'd even

spoken. "Are you fucking serious? How can you even ask me that? It's the reason I didn't tell her sooner. *You* made me keep this a secret, remember? I wanted to be honest, and maybe if I'd been honest earlier, we wouldn't be in this situation."

"Or maybe she would've backed out of the deal sooner."

"Yeah, well, I guess we'll never know now, will we?" Suddenly, the atmosphere in the restaurant was thick, stifling even, and I found myself needing some fresh air. I grabbed my coat and headed for the door.

"Where are you going? You just gonna leave all this for me and Dad?" Corey called.

His question didn't stop me. Nor did I respond to it. Once outside, I waited a minute before putting my jacket on and leaning against the brick exterior.

I found myself wishing I smoked because I would've felt less awkward hanging out on a city street. There was something purposeful about people who stood outside with cigarettes in their hands, like each drag gave them a reason for being there. No one looked at them with suspicious eyes as they walked past, assuming they must be up to no good because no one in their right mind would willingly stand outside on a fifteen-degree night.

But I wasn't one of those people. A woman walked by, moving her bag to the arm closer to the street as her gaze darted to me and then quickly away again. *I'm not* that *much of an asshole*, I wanted to say.

I felt lost, like no matter where I was, I shouldn't be there. I couldn't go back inside and face Corey and my dad, who no doubt heard us arguing from the kitchen but chose not to intervene. And I couldn't just go home, because, as Corey had so appropriately pointed out, I'd be leaving them on their own to do something I'd promised I'd help with. I was a better man than that.

Preparing to go back inside, I took a few more breaths, letting the frigid air fill my lungs before releasing it again. I wished I could release the stress of all of this just as easily. I was about to go back in when the door opened.

"I don't wanna talk about it, Cor," I said.

"Too bad" was the reply, but it wasn't Corey. My dad put his hand on the back of my neck and massaged it roughly like he used to after we lost a baseball game. It occurred to me that he hadn't done that in so long that this was probably the first time he had to reach up instead of down. "We're gonna talk, or at least *I* am. As long as you're listening, I don't really give a shit whether you reply."

He released my neck and positioned himself next to me against the wall. I was thankful we weren't facing each other, because the idea of looking him in the eyes terrified me. Not in a way that instilled actual fear—I'd never had a reason to be scared my father—but in a way that made me scared of my own feelings when I saw the disappointment in his face. I knew that face. I'd seen it when I got caught drinking in high school and when I failed a class my first semester of college. I hadn't seen it since, and I wanted to keep it that way.

"Corey filled me in on what happened," he said, confirming what I already assumed.

I didn't reply because he'd told me I didn't have to, and since I had nothing of value to say, I was more than content to stay silent.

He continued. "You really dug yourself a hole this time."

I rubbed my toe on a crack in the sidewalk and shoved my hands into my pockets after pulling my collar up to block the wind. "I'm sorry," I told him. "If she doesn't buy the restaurant..." I let my sentence remain unfinished because I didn't know how to end it. There wasn't anything I could do to make sure the deal went through, so there was really no point in bringing it up in the first place other than to let my dad know I was more upset about how my fuckup affected his life than how it affected my own.

"She's not."

"What?" I snapped my head up and brought my focus from the ground to meet my dad's eyes, mine already stinging with the tears welling behind them.

"We decided a little while ago that it'd be best if she didn't buy it. She was concerned about how the sale might affect you and...Colton," he said, the beginning of a smirk on his lips, but he managed to control it.

"Wait, so you knew she had us mixed up?"

He nodded.

"And you didn't say anything? To either of us, I mean?"

"Why would I? It's not my business." I was tempted to tell him it absolutely *was* his business, but he continued before I could get my thoughts together. "Plus, I knew you'd tell her soon enough anyway."

"You did?"

"Sure," he said. "I'm actually surprised you didn't tell her earlier. You got way more involved with that poor girl than I'd ever expected you to."

I tried to make sense of his words, but I couldn't. "What does that mean?"

"It means you usually shut the engine off before the bike even has a chance to go anywhere."

"Are you using motorcycle metaphors because you think

I'm too stupid to understand it any other way?"

We both laughed, but it was clear neither of us found the situation funny.

"I'm using a motorcycle metaphor because it's nicer than saying you've sabotaged every relationship that ever had a chance of becoming anything."

His comment surprised me because it wasn't true. At least I didn't *think* it was. "I haven't *sabotaged* anything. Nothing works out, that's all."

"Okay" was all he said, but his tone told me he didn't believe a word I'd said. And something told me the more I thought about what he'd said, the more I wouldn't believe my words either.

"So you're just not gonna sell the restaurant? Or you aren't gonna sell it to Zara? You can't afford to keep it, can you?"

"No, I can't afford to keep it," he answered. "At least not by myself. Which is one of the reasons Zara suggested we go into business together. She figured it would be a good way to let me keep the restaurant in the family and still have her be a part of it. It'll be good for us, and my passion for this place is back."

I was *not* expecting that, though Zara had mentioned that she knew my dad selling the restaurant would be hard for me.

"Well, this is gonna be awkward."

CHAPTER TWENTY-ONE

COLTON

I had likely reached a certain level of stalker as I sat in my car outside Zara's house, but I wanted to talk to her, and I was worried she wouldn't take my call. So here I was. Like a creeper.

This sucked. It shouldn't be like this. I shouldn't feel this baffling mix of excitement and worry to see someone—especially someone I cared about so much. But I needed to man up because someone else I cared about had been dragged into this mess too, and I couldn't let my dad suffer because I was a fuckup.

They'd come to the agreement before we'd fought, so there was no guarantee Zara would still want to be my dad's partner. I threw open my truck door with a burst of purpose, shoved my hands into my pockets, and walked up to her door. I rapped on it quickly before returning my hand to my pocket.

There was a long enough wait to make me question whether she was going to open the door. I knew she was home, or at least strongly suspected it, since her car was out front. But eventually she did open it—just enough to fit herself in the open space.

She looked good—not that that was surprising. She *always* looked beautiful. But in a soft white sweater and tight jeans,

Zara was stunning, and I wished I hadn't lost the right to tell her so.

"What are you doing here?" she asked, not necessarily unkindly but not warmly either. There was a weariness and a wariness to the question that made my insides feel squirrely.

"I needed to talk to you...about the restaurant."

"What about it?" She leaned against the doorjamb and crossed her arms over her chest—the same stance she'd adopted the last time I'd seen her. It was as if she felt she needed to protect herself from me, which made me hurt all over.

"I just want to make sure you know I'll stay out of your way there. I don't want my mistakes to hurt my dad's chances of this deal going through. He seems excited to co-own it with you, and I don't want to cost him that."

She narrowed her eyes. She looked like a praying mantis who was about to eat my head. "So that's what you think of me, huh?"

"Um, what?" What I thought of her? I was worried what she thought of me, sure. But her... She was amazing. How could I ever think anything differently?

"You must think I'm extraordinarily petty if you think I'd compromise not only my own business opportunities but also the chance to work with a man I respect as a business owner and would value as a partner because of my personal feelings about his son."

"Okay, so...that's not even close to what I meant." Jesus, how was it possible I'd fucked this up even worse? Had some warlock put a curse on me or something? Because this was getting ridiculous.

"Then what did you mean?"

"I just didn't want anything that happened with us to

impact how you felt about my dad. He's the best guy I've ever met, and I don't want you to think badly of him just because he raised a moron."

"You're a grown man, Colton. No one is responsible for your decisions except you."

"Yeah. Right. Exactly. Good. Glad we got that settled, then."

She looked at me like I was an idiot, which in her defense was fair. "Goodbye, Colton." And just like that, the door between us was closed.

"Goodbye, Zara," I said softly before returning to my truck. Once inside, I gripped the wheel tightly, as if doing so would keep all the emotions swirling inside me from spilling out of my pores.

When I'd fallen in love with motorcycles in my early twenties, it had been a done deal for me. There'd been no doubt from that point on what I wanted to do for the rest of my life. Even the thought of not working on bikes anymore made my chest feel heavy. Despite my reluctance to commit to things, once I did, it was forever.

And as I sat there with blurry vision and a scratchy throat, I knew the same applied to my feelings for Zara. Forever was a long time to have to live with the heaviness of not being able to have her in my life. And I wasn't sure how I would manage it.

ZARA

Today had sucked. To be fair, all my days since CJ had come clean as Colton had sucked. But seeing him today, looking all sad and sorry, was particularly hard. Especially since he'd only come because he was worried about his dad. Not about me or our relationship.

There had been moments I'd been able to convince myself it hadn't all been a lie. No one was that good an actor—at least some of his feelings for me had to be real. But then I remembered how easily he'd walked away, both a week ago and today, and it cemented how little I knew the real him. How deceived I'd been about who he was.

Because a name was just that: a name. Hadn't Shakespeare written something about names not mattering? A rose would smell sweet no matter what you called it or however the saying went.

If the man behind the name had been real, I maybe could've agreed with that sentiment. I maybe could've gotten past it. And granted, maybe it wasn't the best of odds, but there was a chance. If Colton had only shown that he wanted it. But he hadn't, and he didn't, and that's what had driven me to the *gym*, of all places, on a Wednesday night. Maybe if I worked out hard enough, exhaustion would replace the pain that came from my heart being blown into jagged shards inside my chest.

I walked into Transform Fitness and was immediately greeted with the smiling face of Jaz, one of their trainers. "Zara, you've come to take my hot yoga class. How wonderful."

"I have?" I asked as I scrunched my face up.

"You have," she said purposefully.

"That actually doesn't sound like me." I'd done yoga before, but doing it while sweating to death sounded akin to torture.

"Then maybe you should try sounding like someone else." The teasing was clear in her voice, but her words made me suck in a breath. I'd love nothing more than to *be* someone else—someone who hadn't fallen in love with a liar.

"Okay, I'll give it a try."

"Sweet! Class starts in ten minutes. We have mats outside the studio if you need to borrow one."

I gave her a small smile, said a thank-you I didn't mean, and went to the locker room to lock up my belongings. Since she was drafting people at the front desk, I expected the hot yoga studio to be empty, but it was nearly full. I rolled out my mat in an open space and stretched to keep myself occupied.

A few minutes later, Jaz came in. "No way, you two. I already reserved spots for you up front."

I turned to see who she was talking to, and I noticed the gym owners, Wilder and Maddox, standing on mats in the back corner of the room.

"Come on, Jazzy. We're fine back here," Wilder practically whined. Had he just called her Jazzy?

She pointed a finger at them. "You are going to pay for calling me that in public. And you are most certainly not fine back there. Up front."

"She's so bossy," Wilder mock-whispered. "Who hired her anyway?"

"You did," Maddox grumbled as he started toward the front of the room.

"You let me do the dumbest things." Wilder was shaking his head as if he had deep regret over his choices.

"Keep it up, jokers. You'll regret even signing up for my class."

"You signed us up for this class," Maddox argued as he got settled on the mat Jaz had evidently set up for him at the front of the room.

"Whatever," she said.

"I know what's happening here," Wilder declared. "You're

trying to kill us. Well, your evil plot won't work, Jazzy. The villain never defeats the heroes."

Jaz slowly walked toward him, stepping right into his space. "Did you just refer to *me* as the villain in this scenario?"

Wilder seemed to weigh his next words carefully. "I may have spoken rashly."

Next to him, I could see Maddox smiling widely, clearly enjoying the scene playing out in front of him. I'd suspected for a while there was something more than friendship going on between the three of them, but I didn't know any of them well enough to know for sure. But there was definite chemistry there, and it made me more jealous than it had a right to.

Jaz's stare slowly devolved into a smile. "You're lucky you're cute," she said before moving away from him and getting the class started.

An hour later, I was convinced I'd have been drier if I'd been caught in a rainstorm. But on the plus side, I hadn't thought about Colton during my session. Too bad the effect hadn't lasted longer. Like forever.

At least a portion of my distraction was due to the painful grunts of Maddox and Wilder in the front of the room. It was clear the two large men weren't used to contorting their bodies in graceful ways. They both fell onto their mats and sprawled out like starfish as soon as Jaz announced class was over.

"We survived. We actually survived," Wilder said through harsh pants.

"Speak for yourself," Maddox grunted.

"Get up, drama queens. You need to hydrate," Jaz said as she stood over them, looking amused. She lifted her head and her gaze caught mine, which made me realize I'd been staring.

I quickly wiped down my mat and put it away, waved my

thanks, and hightailed it out of there. After grabbing my stuff, I left the gym, my body enjoying the rush of cold air. Starting toward my car, I found myself hesitating to continue in that direction. I didn't want to go home yet. I didn't want to be social either, so calling any of my friends was out. Noticing a bar a few doors down from the gym, I decided that having a drink in the presence of people I didn't have to actually speak to was appealing.

Walking into Navre's Pub, I took in the dated interior. Light wood floors gave way to green walls. The bar took up an entire wall and had red cushioned stools beside it. I slid onto one, and the bartender immediately came over.

"How ya doing? What can I get ya?"

"Cosmo, please."

He moved away to mix it, and I shucked off my jacket and draped it over the back of my chair. Thankfully I'd worn a long-sleeved shirt over my tank top to the gym, so I felt a little more appropriately dressed than being in completely sweaty workout gear. I removed a twenty from my wallet before putting it back in my small gym bag, which I then attached to the small hook under the bar.

The bartender returned with my drink and asked if he could get me anything else. When I declined, he grabbed the twenty and returned with my change a moment later. I sipped my drink, enjoying the way the fruity flavor slid down my throat and the alcohol warmed my chest. My mind whirled, struggling to latch on to one particular train of thought. Instead, I was being bombarded with a barrage of musings that left me wondering when things were going to get better. As I took another sip of my cocktail, I noticed someone sit on the stool next to mine, even though there were others available.

The bartender came over and tossed a coaster onto the bar. "What can I get ya?"

"Can I get a Miller Lite?" the man beside me said, and the familiarity of his voice made me freeze.

I slowly panned toward the man who'd sat down beside me. *No fucking way.*

From the amused look on his face, I may have said that last bit out loud. "Of all the gin joints in all the world."

Part of me—the panicked part who was losing it at being confronted with the man who looked exactly like his brother and who I'd thought I'd been in a relationship with—wanted to guzzle my drink and run. But the sane part wouldn't allow myself to show that level of weakness. So I ignored him and played with the stem of my glass as though I didn't have a care in the world.

"I'm really glad this isn't awkward," he commented.

I turned to him in disbelief. "I didn't ask you to sit down next to me."

The bartender dropped off Corey's drink but didn't hang around. Corey took a swig from the bottle of lager and then turned his attention back to me.

"What can I say? I'm a glutton for punishment."

He smiled, but it looked all wrong. His canine was slightly crooked, giving his smile a bit of a comedic quality. His eyes were also the wrong shade of green, a little too light to truly pop against eyebrows that were lighter than his brother's. Corey was an attractive man, but it was easy to tell the twins apart once you knew what to look for. That realization actually put me more at ease. I wasn't having a drink with a Colton doppelgänger; I was stuck next to a man I could treat as the stranger he was.

169

"Seems like I'm the one being punished," I muttered as I faced the bar once more.

He chuckled at that and took another drink. The silence between us lasted long enough for me to hope he wasn't going to attempt to hold a conversation. I'd finish my drink and get the hell out of there.

"It was partly my fault," he said, causing my hope to go up in flames. "He wanted to tell you, but I convinced him not to when we found out you were interested in Dad's business. I didn't want the deal to fall through."

I let out a humorless laugh. "You and your brother have very high opinions of me."

"I don't think Colton's ever had a higher opinion of anyone than he does of you."

"Yeah, the months of lying really drove that home."

"Do you really think that?"

"That he has a low opinion of me? Yes."

Corey shook his head. "No, not that part. Though that's bullshit too, for the record. But do you really think he was lying the whole time?"

Narrowing my eyes, I felt my brow furrow. "Uh, yeah. He admitted to it."

"He admitted to letting you think he was me, and sure, I can give you that that wasn't his best moment. But that doesn't mean you didn't get to know who he was."

I rubbed my forehead with my fingers. "Corey, I really don't need this shit right now."

He turned more fully toward me and looked at me intently. "Okay, just please let me say this one thing. Colton is... complicated. He has been for a long time. Who he thinks he is and who he actually is are two very different people. It was like he spent the past ten years being Pinocchio, and then you came along and turned him into a real boy."

"Funny. I see it as the reverse since he's been lying to me since the reunion."

"Shit, I'm fucking this up. It's just..." He took a deep breath before continuing. "I get that he lied about his name, but everything else—how he felt, who he actually *was* when he was with you—that was all real. It was the most real I've seen him be in years. And I hate that I played a part in ruining it for him. Maybe if you guys could just talk—"

I held up a hand to stop him. "We did that. He had his chance to say what he needed to. *Twice*. And none of it hinted at any of the things you just described."

"That doesn't mean they aren't there."

"That may be, but I don't owe him the benefit of the doubt. I don't owe him anything." I stood and grabbed my things.

Corey visibly deflated, probably knowing he couldn't argue it. I had no debts to pay in this situation, and no amount of tugging on my heartstrings was going to change that.

Pushing the stool back so I could slip past him, I said what I hoped would be the last thing I'd ever say to either of them. "If you guys don't want to live with your regrets, don't do things that cause them in the first place."

And with that, I left, wishing this shit day would just end already.

CHAPTER TWENTY-TWO

COLTON

I woke up anxious and frustrated, knowing I had to get out of my apartment. With no real destination in mind, I got in my car and drove. But I wasn't surprised when I pulled up to my dad's house. As I walked in, I felt the constant thrum of anxiety calm a bit. He was my rock, my anchor. And while the negative feelings swirling around my body didn't disappear, they became manageable in my childhood home.

I heard dishes clattering in the kitchen, so I made my way in that direction. My dad must have heard my footfalls, because he was staring at the doorway when I stepped into it. "Morning," he said. "Hungry?"

I wasn't, but I wanted the normalcy that came from him cooking for me in this kitchen. "Yeah. Starved."

He gestured to a stool across the island from where he stood. "Have a seat." He pulled more eggs out of the fridge and set about making me an omelet. A mug of coffee appeared in front of me a minute later.

"Thanks," I said quietly before taking a sip. I hadn't talked to my dad since he'd read me the riot act about lying to Zara, but there was none of the awkwardness I expected.

He plated my eggs and slid them in front of me before tossing me a fork.

"Mom would've yelled at you for throwing utensils in her kitchen."

That made him laugh. "Yeah, she would've. There are a lot of things she would've yelled at me about."

A lump formed in my throat, and I took a big bite of eggs to try to force it down.

"Do you miss it?" I asked, my voice quiet as I looked down at my food.

"Her yelling at me?" he asked with a smile.

It was maybe a weird question to ask, a weird thing to want to know, but it suddenly felt incredibly important to me that I get an answer to it.

He rested his forearms on the island and leaned forward on them. "Yeah, I miss it. I miss everything about her."

"Still?" I asked, finally looking up at him.

He returned my gaze, the look in his eyes intent with honesty. "Every day."

The next question formed on my tongue, but I bit it back. There was no tactful way to ask it, no polite way to phrase it. But it felt like my subconscious had brought me here for answers, and I'd already done a million stupid things. What was one more?

"Was it worth it?"

My dad's brow furrowed. "Was what worth it?"

"Loving her. Was loving her worth the pain of losing her?"

He straightened and ran a hand down his face before he settled his palms on the tile. "Was it for you?"

"She was my mom. Of course it was worth it. And I didn't have a choice but to love her. But you *chose*. And then you lost her, and I just... I need to know, Dad. If you got to do it over again, would you still make the same choice?"

My vision went fuzzy, and I dipped my head a bit to hide the welling in my eyes.

My dad ducked down to catch my gaze with his. "In a heartbeat. She was the love of my life, and she gave me my two boys. Do I wish I got to have her with me for longer? Absolutely. But I have never for a single second regretted loving her, because while being without her hurts, the thought of not having had the chance to love her at all is unbearable."

The tears fell then. I felt them streak down my cheeks as my dad rounded the counter and dragged me to him like he used to when I was a kid. The hug was rough and tight and everything I needed from him. I sank against him and let myself find the comfort I wasn't sure I deserved but needed all the same.

He held me for a minute, and I was able to get myself under control. "When I asked if losing her was worth it for you, I wasn't talking about Mom." His voice was rough in my ear, full of his own emotions, but I didn't pull away. "You gotta ask yourself something, Colton. And be honest. Was letting Zara go the way you did worth how you feel right now? Because you had what your mother and I had, son. Or at least the beginnings of it. And now you have the pain that comes with not having it anymore."

He pulled back and cupped my face in his big hands so I couldn't look away. "But you didn't lose her. You let her go. And that's a difference you're either going to have to live with or do something about." He took a step back. "Eat your eggs."

Wiping my face, I took a deep breath and settled back onto my seat. I scooped up some eggs, but before I brought them to my mouth, I said, "Dad?"

"Yeah?"

And maybe it was odd for the words to make me uncomfortable, but they weren't words we'd exchanged often. They were words we intrinsically knew without them having to be said. But I was coming to learn that a lot of things could get lost in the silence, and there were some things that needed to be made clear before you lost the chance to do so. "I love you."

He smiled. "Love you too, son."

Returning his smile with a small one of my own, I dug into my breakfast, and he started talking about the odds of Brady winning another championship. Things between us had been restored to their factory settings, and it felt good to have one relationship in my life back to the way it should be.

Now I just had to figure out what to do about the other one.

CHAPTER TWENTY-THREE

COLTON

I didn't know what to do with my hands. Or my eyes. And my heart felt like it was beating out of my chest. But in some strange way, it felt like my chest was completely empty, with no heart at all. Zara would probably agree with that.

I was scared to death of what might happen over the next few minutes. It wasn't that I was afraid to tell her how I really felt. It was what her reaction would be that had my palms sweating and my throat dry. I guzzled part of a bottle of water before setting it back in the cup holder and shutting off the ignition.

My dad had told me Zara would be at the restaurant getting a few things ready before the grand reopening this weekend, and I was hoping that meant she couldn't just take off if she didn't want to see me. I told myself I'd respect her wishes if she asked me to leave, but I honestly didn't know if I'd be able to if it came to that. At least not without saying what I wanted to say. I'd given up without a fight, and if my last two interactions with Zara were any indication, I'd better be ready for one.

I zipped my jacket up to my chin and jogged toward the front door, hoping like hell it was open. If it was locked, I was fairly certain Zara wasn't going to open it once she knew who stood on the other side. I pulled lightly and sighed in relief when it opened. I could see Zara toward the back, sitting at the bar with her back to the door. She didn't turn around, so she must not have heard me. She was obviously too distracted by the music playing through a Bluetooth speaker behind the bar and the paperwork she was studying in front of her.

I watched her for a length of time more appropriate for a lion hunting unsuspecting prey than for a human to stare at another person without their knowledge. If I'd felt like a stalker before, I was pretty sure this visit might result in a restraining order.

I managed to sit a few seats down from her without her looking my way, and again my hands couldn't find a place they felt comfortable. I rubbed my thighs and cracked my knuckles and pushed my hands in and out of my jacket pockets. I wasn't sure if I cleared my throat as a way of alerting her to my presence or if it was another nervous tic, but when she heard me, she startled for a moment before realizing it was me. And then she looked back down at her papers.

"Your dad's not here." She picked up a pretzel from a bowl beside her and placed it into her mouth.

"I know. I came to see you. Third time's the charm, I'm hoping." I laughed softly, but it was absent of any real humor. She didn't laugh, and that didn't surprise me. "Can we talk?"

She set her pen down and straightened her posture in a way that came across as professionally distant, giving me a glimpse into what all future interactions might look like now that she worked with my father. "I honestly don't know what there is to talk about." She didn't sound angry. She sounded like she was stating a simple fact. "I've said everything I need to say."

"But I haven't," I replied, my voice urgent with the need to speak before she stopped me or I lost the courage to do so.

Like I had, she laughed, but hers sounded more disgusted than awkward. Her lips were tight—her expression filled with something I couldn't describe other than to say it made my insides feel all icky.

I'd planned this conversation so many times in my mind over the past twenty-four hours. What I wanted to say, how I wanted to say it, possible responses to her replies, if she even chose to reply to any of it. But never in my imaginary scenario had I begun our conversation how I did. "Do you know what I like best about having a twin?"

She was silent for a moment. "The fact that you can impersonate each other whenever it's convenient for you?"

"I deserved that."

"No shit you did." If I didn't know she still despised me, I would've thought I recognized a lightness to her voice I hadn't heard since our breakup. But I knew better than to point it out.

"I deserve a lot of things," I said. "I deserve your anger and your hate. I deserve to be called a liar and any other horrible word you can think to call me. The only thing I don't deserve is you."

She looked over at me, holding my stare, which I didn't dare let go.

"But that doesn't mean I won't fight for you anyway."

"I don't *hate* you," she said.

Her comment comforted me more than it probably should have.

"I've been miserable without you, Zar. I'm sick because of it. And even though it's completely selfish of me to ask you to give me a second chance, I can't just let you walk away. Not again." I felt like I'd let all of that out without taking a breath, so I inhaled deeply to replace the oxygen that seemed to be missing from my lungs.

She sighed and popped another pretzel into her mouth. "What is it you love about having a twin?"

I'd forgotten I'd asked the question, but I knew the answer anyway. "It's that I have someone who knows me better than anyone else does. Someone who can finish my sentences and will call me out on my bullshit."

"How nice for you," she said, not bothering to hide the sarcasm in her voice.

"I'm telling you this because, before you...before *we* had whatever it was we had, the only person I felt that way about was Corey. I could never imagine having a connection with someone else like that, and I never wanted to." I thought I saw her eyes soften a bit, but it was difficult to tell in the dim light. "I know I told you it didn't matter what my name was because you knew the real me, but I realize now that's not true. You don't know the real me. Not completely, anyway."

She tensed, pressing her lips together before she said, "You know what? On second thought, I don't even want to hear whatever it is you're about to say. I've heard enough of your lies. I'm done with all of it." She waved her hand, dismissing me and anything else I planned on sharing.

"I love you," I blurted out. "And that's not a lie. Not even close to one. If I'm being honest, I've loved you for a while, but I was too much of a chickenshit to tell you. You want to know who I really am? I'm a coward and I'm selfish, and I make one bad decision after another." I nervously brushed some imaginary lint off my pants.

"Keep going."

"I should've told you I wasn't Corey that first night, but I didn't, and I can't change that. In typical Colton Jensen fashion, I dug myself a hole I couldn't climb out of. And I didn't want to, because telling you the truth could've meant not only losing my dad's deal, it could've meant losing you."

"But you told me eventually anyway," Zara said softly. I could tell none of it made any sense to her, and she was right for being confused. It had made no sense to me either until my talk with my dad. "And you still lost me."

"I'm trying to change that."

"Keep trying," she said.

I had a chance, though probably not a good one. "I was scared you'd leave, so I pushed you away. You said you wanted to know who I really was, but it's better off you didn't. I'm an asshole who has no idea how to be in a relationship because I never thought I wanted one. I was terrified to have one. I watched my dad lose the love of his life—someone he loved for twenty years—and he hasn't been the same since. I can't imagine going through that." My gaze locked with Zara's, and she looked like she was fighting back tears. "So I pushed away the best thing that ever happened to me before I could love you more than I already did. Because any more time with you would only make the inevitable end that much more difficult."

Zara was quiet. Thankfully she didn't look angry anymore. Just sad.

"I'm not asking you to pick up where we left off. It would be naïve of me to think we could."

"Then what *are* you asking?" I thought I saw her expression fall a bit, like my admission disappointed her more than I already had.

"I'm asking you to give me a chance to start again—to do

it right from the beginning this time. And if it doesn't work out, then I guess we really aren't meant to be together. But I want to try." My voice was soft, my eyes pleading. "I want you to *let* me try."

She shook her head, but it seemed more out of doubt than refusal. "How do we just start again?"

She'd opened the door a crack. Now all I needed to do was push it open enough to fit through it. I gave her a shy smile. "Do I know you? You look so familiar, but I can't figure out where we've met."

It took her a moment to realize what I was doing, but I could tell when she did because a lopsided smile played at the edge of her lips. She leaned her elbow on the bar and propped her head up in her hand as she looked at me. "I think we went to high school together."

"Yes!" I pointed at her excitedly. "Zara Pierce. I remember now. You're so much more beautiful than I remember. Gorgeous," I added softly.

"I was a bit of a nerd in high school." It could've been wishful thinking, but I thought I saw her move a little closer to me.

"And I was an arrogant prick who only cared about myself."

Releasing her head from her hand, she smiled. "Now see, if you had introduced yourself like that at the reunion, I would've known you were Colton immediately."

"I'm trying to be serious here," I said, though my laugh told her otherwise. I was sincere, but the fact that she was joking with me flooded my veins with a relief I never expected to feel.

"Sorry," she said. "Continue."

I extended my hand to her, and I relaxed even more when she took it. It had been too long since I'd touched her. "Colton Jensen," I said. "It's nice to see you again."

"Nice to see you again too, Colton. Seems like I'm not the only one who's changed a lot since high school."

"No," I said. "You're not."

ZARA

Until he'd come into the restaurant, I hadn't realized how much I'd truly missed him. But I'd had time to think about all of it, to accept that a part of the misunderstanding—albeit a very tiny part—had been my fault. And even though the continuation of the misunderstanding—lie—had been CJ's fault, the truth was, just like him, I'd been miserable since we split. I could tell he was trying desperately to hold back a grin as he brought my hand up to his lips. When he released it, I missed his touch immediately. I needed it again, needed more of him this time.

"I'm not usually this forward," I said, "but would it be okay if I kissed you?"

He brought his hand up to my cheek and gently stroked it with his thumb. "It'd be more than okay. It'd be perfect."

And with that, our lips found the other's, and somehow we were right back to where we were, no longer in the roles of virtual strangers who'd reconnected at a bar. We were CJ and Zara, two people who loved each other but were terrified to tell the other.

"I was scared too," I said, pulling away between breathless kisses.

"Of what?" His lips found my neck after removing my

shirt, and they worked down my body from my collarbone to my breasts.

"Of this," I said. "Of loving someone so fully I can't be without them. I was worried about what it would do to my career. To my life," I added. CJ's mouth made my head fuzzy, and it was getting more and more difficult to think straight.

His attention to my chest was interrupted when he brought his gaze up to meet mine. "You love me?" he asked. "You don't just need to say that because I did."

"CJ?" I said. "Colton?" His name tasted good on my tongue, sweet and rough like the man himself. "No more lies, remember? We're done with those. If I say I love you, it's because I mean it."

His smile beamed for a moment before he lowered his head and I couldn't see his face anymore. Once we were both naked, we looked for any available surface to make up for the time we missed while we were apart. I wrapped my legs around him as he held me up, kissing my neck and carrying me to the edge of the bar to set me on top of it. It wasn't long before he was hovering over me too, lining himself up and pressing into me.

I dug my nails into his back as he pumped into me, both of us racing to the end because we knew this was only the beginning. We could do this again and again, forever. And forever sounded like a perfect amount of time.

Neither of us spoke aloud. Our eyes and actions said more than any words could've. We'd talked enough, and now wasn't a time to talk. So we let our heavy breaths and racing heartbeats tell the other we were getting close. And when we finally came, it was a release like one I'd never felt before.

Colton kissed me, a slow and lingering kiss, before

climbing off me and the bar and helping me down. We headed to the bathrooms to clean up.

"We can never tell your dad we had sex on his bar," I said.

"It's your bar too now," CJ said. "We'll just tell him we stayed on your half of it."

My jaw dropped before I realized he was kidding.

He laughed. "Or we'll just Lysol the hell out of it and hope no one notices."

"Sounds like a plan."

EPILOGUE

COLTON

Two years later...

I slid my hand from Zara's lower back, stopped walking, and turned to face her. She stopped with me. Silently, I took in the glow of her skin, the way her hair fell softly over her shoulders, how beautiful she looked. For a moment, my attention focused on the pendant she wore around her neck—the one I'd never thought I'd take off mine—and I wondered how I'd gone my whole life trying to resist this feeling. It was absolutely perfect.

I took her hand and brought it up to my lips for a kiss. "You ready for this?" I asked before turning toward the restaurant again and beginning to walk slowly.

"I'm excited. What about you?"

"Excited is one word for it." I could sense her staring at me more than I could see it. "I'm kidding. It'll be fun." I hoped, anyway. Gender reveals weren't normally on my agenda, and the few I'd been to had been less than enthralling, but of course this one would be different because it was *our* baby.

Once inside, we were greeted by our family and friends. Zara's mom gave me a kiss on the cheek, even though I'd just seen her a few days prior. And her father shook my hand before pulling me into a hug.

"How's my grandson doing?" he asked, and I had to laugh.

Both our families had been texting us possible names and using gender-specific pronouns for weeks, hoping to get us to slip up. But we were a vault that couldn't be cracked. Corey even took me out for way too many beers, and somehow I'd still managed to keep it a secret.

"Nice try," I said to Zara's father. "You'll find out soon enough."

"Fine, fine," he replied, and again I couldn't help but think the reason we were all here was a result of me banging his daughter. I hoped the thought hadn't crossed his mind as often as it had crossed mine. It'd made things awkward as hell.

"Let's cut the cake now," Meemaw called from across the room. She was approaching us holding two gifts that she struggled to see over.

"Grandma, you didn't have to bring us anything. I'll have a shower when it gets closer."

"Nonsense," she said as she let go of the presents and allowed me to take them. "And they aren't for *you*. They're for the baby. Don't tell me I can't get my great-grandchild something when I want to. That baby'll be spoiled if I have a say in it."

Zara rolled her eyes and said a genuine thank-you to Meemaw before giving her a kiss on her wrinkled cheek. "Is it okay if we open them a little later?"

"Did you not hear me just tell you they aren't yours? When the baby comes, she can open them."

"I doubt a newborn will be able to open these," I said. "And how do you know the baby's a girl?"

Meemaw laughed like the question was a ridiculous one before excusing herself to get some food, which we insisted everyone else do as well before it was time to cut the cake. The suspense was killing everyone as they helped themselves to roast beef, meatballs, salad, and some sides prepared by the chef at Maggie's. People nibbled on cookies, including Zara, who'd developed a sweet tooth she'd never had before the pregnancy.

"Who's hungry for some cake?" my dad said, already holding the box he'd picked up from the bakery for us. Zara had ordered the cake and knew the owner, who had sworn to keep the secret just that. My dad set the box down on the table in the middle of the room and looked to the two of us. "Can we open it?" he asked, looking like a kid at his birthday party.

I looked to Zara.

"I'm okay with it if you are," she said.

Hoping my smile answered for me, I put my arm around her and gave her a kiss on her forehead. Then I lifted the lid of the box and handed Zara the knife.

"Wait, where's Brielle?" she asked, standing on her toes to see over the surrounding people.

Devon brought a beer to his lips and said, "I think one of the girls spilled something on herself, and Brielle's changing her."

We waited a few more minutes for Brielle, which meant we had to listen to Zara's cousin Joel tell us that gender reveals were becoming less popular due to people's hesitance to assign their child a gender before birth. At a loss for any words that wouldn't further his explanation, I managed to provide a "Huh, interesting."

Meemaw looked confused, but luckily Brielle appeared with their youngest daughter before the older woman had a chance to ask Joel to elaborate.

Zara made a show out of letting the knife cut through the white icing slowly before she pulled out the first piece to reveal the pink cake inside. The room filled with laughter, screams, and some excited cursing from my brother.

Once things quieted down a bit, Joel asked, "So is it a girl or a boy?"

"A girl," pretty much everyone answered.

Becca and Trinity nearly squealed with delight. "I can't wait to buy her a bunch of cute pink outfits," Trinity said.

"I asked because in the eighteen hundreds, pink was a masculine color," Joel added. "Many boys wore pink because the men wore red and boys are just little men. Girls were actually the ones who wore blue much of the time."

"Shut up, Joel," Meemaw said. "So do you have a name picked out yet, or are you keeping that one a secret too?"

Zara and I looked at each other before I said, "No, *that* we'll share. She's gonna be Maggie."

My dad came over immediately and hugged us both, and the tears in his eyes were the first ones I'd ever seen there. "I'm so happy for you guys," he said. "You'll be amazing parents." He'd told me so many times I'd make a wonderful father, and it was difficult to agree because I'd never pictured myself as one. The only thing that made me believe him was that *he* was a great father, so I figured he might be a good judge. "Oh, before I forget, your friend at the bakery gave me another box, Zara. He didn't charge you for that one. Said it's his gift to you two."

"That's nice. We should've put it out earlier," I said. "It's probably cookies or something."

"No, he told me to wait to open it until you opened the cake box."

"I'll grab it." I headed to the kitchen and brought it out,

cutting the tape with my fingers. When I lifted the lid, I was surprised by the contents. "Why would he give us another cake?" I asked. "There aren't that many people here."

Zara pressed her lips together before letting them slide into a smile. "Because it's for the second baby," she said slowly, quietly, like she was scared for my well-being.

My eyes widened, and I found myself getting light-headed. "I think I need to sit down." How the hell had I not known there were two babies? I'd missed *one* appointment when I'd come down with a stomach bug, but Zara hadn't mentioned anything to me when she'd gotten home. "Are you serious? Two? We're having two babies? At once?"

She nodded, and the rest of the room was silent. Or at least it felt that way. "Maybe this wasn't the best way for me to tell you, but when I found out, you were sick, and I didn't think the news would make you feel any better. Then I thought it would be a fun surprise." She shrugged like she'd been withholding a small gift from me instead of life-changing news.

"It's a surprise, all right. The fun part is yet to be determined."

"Ha!" My dad laughed loudly. "Twins. Who would've guessed? I always thought they skipped a generation."

"I always thought that too," Zara said. "But apparently the egg can split at any time, which is what happened in my case, which also means—"

"It's a girl," I said so softly I wasn't even sure if I'd actually vocalized it.

"It's a girl," Zara repeated.

The room was still silent. Whether they were waiting to see if they needed to call 9-1-1 or they were just unsure of how to react, I wasn't sure.

"So I'm gonna have twin girls," I said more to myself than anyone else. And then I imagined it. Holding two little babies, both in pink, my fingers in their tiny, fragile hands as I rocked them; dropping two small girls off at kindergarten and hoping no boys chased them on the playground; walking each one down the aisle on their wedding day. And suddenly I couldn't picture my life without them.

And as I looked at my wife gazing lovingly at me, I realized that if it was my destiny to be surrounded by beautiful, kind women, then my life turned out pretty much perfect. But our daughters better not try to date twin boys. That shit was definitely not happening.

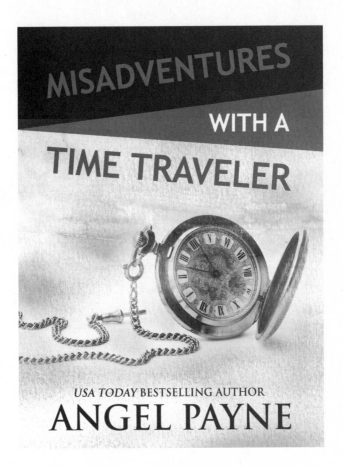

EXCERPT FROM

MISADVENTURES WITH A TIME TRAVELER

Where is a stud like Christophe when I need him? How long has it been since I've relaxed enough to think about straddling a hot-blooded hunk like him? A French one, at that. Not that my life gives me time to be a hussy, but my one experience with a French lover was absolutely one to remember. Filthy words. Filthier moves. Worked for my multiple orgasms like an Eagle Scout going for a merrit badge.

I laugh at that only because sobbing is the alternative. Which is stupid, because the last year of my life has been one of its best. In the fashion-influencer arena, I'm no longer in the grandstands. While I'm not center stage yet, I'm at least headed toward it.

Yes...sacrifices have been made.

Lots of them.

Like being alone some nights. Hornier than hell. Ready to hump the bedpost for some relief.

But I'm not sorry about any decisions I've made to get here.

No. Not sorry.

But maybe a little of something else.

Feelings I don't allow myself to visit often—but right now, in this place and on this occasion, maybe the emotional expedition is necessary.

I cross to the window as if the decision itself draws me. I grab the window latch and twist, pushing the pane open.

It's a chilly but clear March night, with a light wind skittering small leaves across the gardens. Moonlight turns everything silver. The effect is heightened as the sprinklers come on, their spray turning into stars on the breeze before landing on the garden's Grecian statues. The water courses down all the inert, elegant faces. They're shedding the tears that I can't.

That I won't.

Displaying vulnerability won't change a thing. I'll still be standing at a window in the middle of the night, identifying with garden statues to distract from the shit that's really gnawing at me.

That sometimes, during the nights in which it's too quiet to ignore the thrum of my heart, I have to let it speak to the rest of me.

To tell me it's alone.

No. Not just alone.

Lonely.

The certainty is like silver-cold moonlight across my blood and bones. My sugar rush vanishes. My head starts to throb. So does the triangle between my thighs.

What the hell is wrong with me?

"Buzzed," I mumble. "You're buzzed, honey. And tired. Ohhh, so tired." I swing my head around, focusing on the grand production that is my bed. "Yeah. Time for sleep, wenchie Allie."

With the hope that Christophe will stop by to fulfill a birthday fantasy, I decide to go commando under my long sleep tee. A long moan breaks free as I free my chest from my bra. *Nothing* beats that bliss.

Well...one thing might.

The recognition is only a few seconds old before I wrap one hand around a carved bedpost, and let the other drift to the cleft between my thighs. A sigh spills out as my pussy comes alive. So good. Ohhh shit, this feels *so* damn good. When was the last time I did even this for myself? Weeks, at least.

Weeks.

No wonder my body all but screams at me to keep up the fun. No wonder I answer with higher gasps and quickening rubs.

I fall back onto the bed and let my legs dangle over the side of the plush mattress. I spread my thighs, exposing more for my fingers to touch...and arouse. I emit a longer moan while palming my breasts through my T-shirt. Squeezing them. Pinching them. Hardening them.

Vaguely, I realize that Dmitri was probably brazen enough to pack my vibrator too. At this point, not worth it to look. I'm too far-gone to stop. With tight, fast circles, I work my frantic fingertips over my tingling clit. Faster still. Faster. I sigh and hum and mewl. Groan and gulp and growl.

Yes.

I'm almost there.

So close.

Almost...there.

Damn it. Yesssss...

Wait.

What the hell?

I sit up. Hold my breath. I'm not the only one generating

sound in this room.

What on earth is going on?

Who's making all those strange, soft hums? And where are they making them?

I swallow hard, forcing myself to look at the towering wardrobe in the corner. The pachyderm of a cabinet is stunning but daunting. Its front panels are testaments to the craftsmen of centuries past, inlaid with mother-of-pearl pictures. Naked angels are dancing with moonbeams in different shades of the shiny nacre. But that's the extent of my observation about the handiwork of the thing for now. I'm mesmerized—hypnotized—by the wardrobe for a different reason.

Because...

"Holy. Shit."

Is the damn thing...calling to me? *Singing to me?*

The sound, a bizarre blend of electrical resonance and a harpsichord melody, is like no music I've ever heard. The song has no structure or rhythm but compels me like a symphony written solely for my spirit. No part of me can ignore it.

"What...the..."

I can't finish because the chest suddenly starts to shake.

My heart thunders with primal terror, yet I scoot to my feet and walk toward the damn thing.

Pulled by the golden light that glows from behind the eight-foot doors...

Light?

"Oh, my God," I rasp. "Okay, Allie. You are seriously drunk or damn deranged." I hope for the former but suspect the latter. With every step I take, the suspicion intensifies.

I reach for the one of the wrought-iron handles. I'm dazzled by the sunlight still effusing from beyond, consuming the silhouettes of my fingers.

I pull the door open.

And at once am tackled by the sun.

All right, the human version of it.

But before I can scream, he grabs both sides of my face. He locks my stare with the amber force of his. I gasp as he holds me tight. Tighter. But I still don't scream. Why? Holy shit, why am I not shrieking like the horror-movie girl dumb enough to take a midnight swim in the lake?

He's two thoughts ahead. He stretches his thumbs in, pressing them over my mouth, trapping me from bursting with sound. Once more, he drenches me in his melted-sun gaze. There's a wild, desperate expression across his chiseled features. He doesn't relent the ferocity, as if he's been chained inside that armoire since the century it was made.

Beautiful.

The syllables are an aria in my mind, exquisite and unending.

He's so heart-stoppingly beautiful.

Thick, chestnut-colored hair tumbles around his bold but elegant face, some of it covering an inch-long scar over his left eye. But most of the mane is secured at his nape with a crafted leather thong. He's wearing a fitted brocade vest over a white linen shirt that has ties and ruffles instead of seams and buttons. His V-shaped torso and long, braced legs are as commanding as his linebacker-wide shoulders.

Wow.

Wow.

No wonder I keep questioning the reality of all this.

Because with this reality, who the hell needs fantasy?

Drue and Raegan must have chosen this guy as a naughty birthday gift. I wouldn't think there'd be many male dancers around these parts, but I'm not asking questions or complaining. He makes Christophe look like a five or six to his solid ten on the Gods of Loire scale.

"Mon Dieu. Mon Dieu, c'est un miracle."

Holy *crap*. His *voice*.

Every syllable drenches my blood like rich wine. It's liquid velvet infused with the strength of the earth. It harmonizes perfectly with the soft song in my head.

Happy birthday to me...

Happy birthday to me...

"Okay." I smile to let him know screaming isn't on my immediate agenda. "I'll go with miracle if that's your jam, gorgeous."

When he tucks his eyebrows together, I notice other awesome things about his face. A couple of rugged nicks, besides the larger gouge, in his forehead. The luxurious length of his lashes. The stunning imbalance of his mouth, with the lower lip bigger than the top.

I wonder what his story is. He's probably some local kid working the family vineyard during the day and taking gigs like this for some extra cash at night. Who am I to fault him? Rough times call for strange measures.

Finally, he murmurs, "You...are British."

"Close." I play with his shirt ruffles, just to sneak my fingers against a little of the chest beneath. Chiseled. Hard. *Beautiful.* There's real power beneath his strength. "I'm American. Your people didn't tell you that?"

"No." He sounds like he's choking as I trail my fingers along his collarbones. "There was little time. My God, that feels incredible."

He pushes closer, gliding his hands down my sides and over my hips. He caresses me with reverence, as if trying to memorize me.

Wow.

"That's what this is all about, right?" I slip my hands to the back of his neck, giving in to the moment with subtle sways of my hips. "Feeling good?" I jog my head toward the wardrobe. "Getting the hell out of there?" I refrain from asking why he took so long to pop out, since he's clearly been staged for this entrance since we finished up dessert. Probably longer. But with that in mind, who am I to call the guy out for catching a catnap? Now that he's rested, I don't have to worry about wearing him out.

"Hell." Shadows take over his face as he echoes the word. "An apt description." Just as quickly, he violently shakes his head. "But it no longer matters." His eyes are sunrise-gold again. "You are what matters."

Oh, damn. He's good. Did they give him the romance bestsellers' list as training material? It's working. His reverent touch makes me sizzle. His powerful presence brings my libido fully back online. If I'm not careful, I'll let this hunk do more than take off his clothes for me.

He cups my face again. "My miracle. You are real. You are here."

"Errrm...yeah." I'm tempted to leave it at that, especially when he dips his big gorgeous head and leans his brow against mine. But I manage to add, "Here is...definitely... where I'm at."

"I did not believe it." He lowers his long fingers to the sides of my neck. "When she told me it would be so. I did not believe."

"And that's why you stayed in there so long?"

"Too long." He presses his fingertips into my nape. Holy crap, does it feel good. His touch is so warm and strong and earnest. "I should have believed...so much sooner..."

"But you do now." I forced some casual cheer into it. "And I'd really love to get this show on the road. So shall we? Or should I say...shall you?"

I step back, but he catches me by the wrist, yanking me close again. "The road? Where are you going? And in the middle of the night? The moon is still high."

"Oh, my God. You're cute." I stop my giggle when he doesn't break character, even given that permission. "All right, Marquis de Hunkville, we'll do this your way." I glance back into the wardrobe, despite the tick that goes off in his jaw as I do. "Did you bring music to get your groove on?"

"Pardon moi?"

"Where are your hot licks, hot stuff?" I reward myself for the wit by looking him over again. His historical culottes don't leave a lot of his lower physique to my imagination; an accurate-looking eighteenth-century fly conceals a breathtaking crotch and tree trunk thighs. Handcrafted riding boots are filled by his massive calves. Holy hell, he's well-built. "Maybe you just play the music from your phone?" I venture. "Or maybe you don't dance at all. There's...a lot of you, after all."

"My...what? Foam?" He huffs. "What does a steed's spittle have to do with playing music? Though I can certainly play a few tunes if you would like some entertainment, my love." He steps back and extends an elbow. "Will you allow me to escort you to the conservatory?"

"I'd prefer to stay right here." The confession stuns me as much as it does him. I mean, there's historically accurate, and then there's calling a client *my love*. Hell to the no. "If you need, I've got some curated lists saved to my laptop. Probably better than trying your mobile anyhow. The connectivity in this place is sketchy at best."

"You...are saving *what* atop your lap?"

"Never mind." I laugh again, trying to play off how nice it feels to have him gawking at my midsection. More than that, observing the fresh transition of his gaze. Sunrise to sunset in five seconds flat. "So no music. Good enough." I channel my inner siren, who feels close to a goddess now, to steer us back toward lighter stuff. "Maybe...you'll just let me help, then."

"Help? With wh—" He erupts in a shocked snarl as I slide a finger along his waistband—and then lower. "My *God*. My love, what are you about?"

"Same thing you're about, Hunkville." I twist a couple of his buttons free. His hard flesh swells against my touch, and once more he's my blazing sun. "But knock it off with 'my love,' okay? My name is Allie. Alessandra works if you want to keep it foofy and formal. Think of ways to say either of those while we get you naked, yeah?"

This story continues in
Misadventures with a Time Traveler!

ACKNOWLEDGMENTS

We of course have to thank Meredith Wild for liking our writing enough to bring us onto the Misadventures team. You've been a friend to us since the beginning, and we're eternally grateful for that.

To Scott, Robyn, and the editing team, thank you for all of your hard work and kind words. You're so great at what you do, and you're a pleasure to work with.

To the rest of the Waterhouse Press team, thank you for your continued support and for designing all of the kickass covers and graphics.

The Padded Room, thank you for supporting our craziness. From posting links, teasers, and helping get our name out there, you are a vital part of our dreams. We love you ladies!

To our families, we're not sure how all of you put up with us so we can keep riding along on this journey, but we love you for that and a million other reasons. Thank you :)

MORE MISADVENTURES